THE QUIET AMISH BACHELOR

SEVEN AMISH BACHELORS BOOK 5

SAMANTHA PRICE

MARY LOU STARED at Taylor's house as her taxi stopped out front. It certainly was grand. She'd heard that the girl her future brother-in-law was involved with was from a wealthy family and whoever had told her that hadn't been exaggerating.

Even though Mary Lou was marrying Jacob in a few days and should've been concentrating on her wedding, she figured the greatest gift she could give Jacob and his family was to reunite Timothy with his estranged girlfriend, especially considering that Taylor was carrying his child. While Timothy was on *rumspringa* he'd managed to get himself into one sticky situation after another, and Mary Lou wanted to help.

"Is this the house, Mary Lou?"

Mary Lou was irritated by her cousin's whining voice. Her mother had invited Magnolia back to their home to help with the wedding. By the time Mary Lou found out *Mamm* had done that, it was too late to stop her. For the last few days, Magnolia had insisted on going everywhere with Mary Lou. She was becoming like a shadow—a relentless shadow—from which Mary Lou could not escape. "This is the address I found. Come on, we must get this out of the way, so we can do something else this afternoon."

"It looks very opulent; like a palace almost."

"*Jah,* all the houses around here are like that, if you hadn't noticed."

They both got out of the taxi and once Mary Lou had paid the driver, Magnolia said, "I don't know why you're wasting our time. It's disgraceful, what he did, and he's an embarrassment to his family." Magnolia shook her head. "Timothy got this girl pregnant and I don't know that you should be sticking your beak in where things don't concern you. It's his problem and he should deal with it and clean up his own mess."

Beak? Mary Lou was tempted to point out that with Magnolia's plain looks, she shouldn't be calling her nose a beak, but Mary Lou had turned a new leaf and was doing her best to be nice to others. After all, God had blessed her with the nicest, most handsome man in the community, so it was her duty to be uplifting toward people, even Magnolia. "For your information, Magnolia, Timothy will soon be my *bruder*-in-law and it won't be an embarrassment to the family when Timothy marries this girl."

"But, she doesn't want to marry him. She's not going to change her mind because you talk to her."

"That's not the point, but yes, you're right, that's what she said. You're forgetting that people change their minds all the time. I have to try something." Mary Lou had no idea why her mother thought Magnolia should stay at their place before and during her wedding. The worst part of it was she had no choice but to have Magnolia tag along with her everywhere she went. It was the only way to avoid a lecture from her mother about learning to get along with others. The last time Magnolia had visited, her cousin had left after they'd had a tiff.

"What makes you think she'll even be home?" Magnolia scrunched her nose, staring up at the mansion.

"Well, I don't know, do I? I'll knock on the door and see if she's at home. If she's not, I'll come back later." Frowning at Magnolia, she said, "This is something I must do alone. She won't feel at all comfortable if two of us show up. You walk up the street and back. I'll wait right here for you when I'm done."

"You want me to walk up and down?"

"*Jah.*"

"*Nee.* I want to come too."

Mary Lou chuckled and shook her head. There was no way she was letting that happen. "*Nee.* I already told you that you could come in the taxi with me, but you can't come in." When she looked at the way Magnolia's lips were compressed into a thin white line that emphasized her square jaw, she tried to soften the blow. "How about when we finish here I'll take you to lunch? My treat."

Magnolia's lips relaxed. "Okay. Can we go to that diner near the park?"

"Okay. They make the best chocolate shakes."

"*Denke.* I'd like that."

"Me too. Well, off you go." Mary Lou shooed her away with her hands.

Magnolia turned away and dawdled up the street, and then turned around.

Mary Lou had stood there watching just in case Magnolia changed her mind about what they'd just decided. "When I'm finished I'll come out and wait right here." Mary Lou pointed to the ground where she stood. When Magnolia nodded and turned back around and started walking, Mary Lou was more than a little relieved that Magnolia hadn't further insisted upon coming with her to talk with Taylor. It would need great tact and diplomacy, talking to a stranger about such a delicate subject.

Pushing some loose strands of hair away from her face, Mary Lou forged ahead. She stepped onto the long driveway and walked along the center as the small white pebbles crunched beneath her feet. There were none of the high fences or security gates that Mary Lou had expected around a home such as this.

She knocked on the door. When there was no

answer she knocked again. Just when she was about to walk away, she heard someone talking. The voice came from the other side of the house. She followed the sound and soon saw Taylor through the walls of a glasshouse. She was holding a pink watering can, looking much the same as when she'd seen her talking to Jacob. Taylor was watering some plants with one hand, while with the other she held a cell phone up to her ear.

Mary Lou continued walking toward her. When Taylor looked up and saw her, she immediately ended her call and stepped to the doorway.

"Are you a friend of Timothy's?" The girl asked as soon as they were face to face.

"That's right. I'm Mary Lou. Soon to be his sister-in-law."

"Did he send you here?"

Mary Lou shook her head. "No, not at all. He'd likely be furious if he knew I was here."

Taylor set the watering can down.

"I was hoping we could talk?"

Taylor nodded. "Okay." Then, looking back at the plants, she said, "My mother has gone away and I'm looking after her orchids. They're not mine. I'm not a plant person."

"Oh." Mary Lou couldn't work out why Taylor said that. Was she too cool for plants? She was a pretty girl with her dark hair swept up into a casual topknot and wearing designer ripped jeans. Her tee shirt was long and loose-fitting, stopping at her hips. Mary Lou knew the long shirt was to hide her growing belly.

"What did you want to say to me?"

Mary Lou thought fast. She had half expected the girl would send her away without listening to anything she said. Mary Lou licked her lips. "I was wondering if you would want to come to my wedding. I'm marrying Timothy's brother, Jacob."

"Oh, you're marrying Jacob?"

"That's right." Mary Lou nodded.

Taylor pulled a face and Mary Lou hoped that meant she was thinking about it. It wasn't an expression that said, 'No way!' Maybe Taylor remembered her. She had once interrupted Jacob when he was speaking with her. That was several weeks ago.

Taylor turned around and went back to watering the orchids with the long-spouted watering can. "I don't even know if I'm watering them correctly. I've got an idea that I'm not supposed to water them from the top. She told me but I wasn't listening. I hope they don't die before my mother comes home. That'd give her another reason to hate me."

"Yes. That would be terrible." Mary Lou stepped inside the glass greenhouse with Taylor.

"Tell me about it. When are you getting married?"

"In a week, on the twenty fourth."

"And I'm guessing that Timothy is going, too?"

It didn't occur to Mary Lou that it would be awkward for Taylor to come to the wedding alone if

Timothy didn't come, but then again, maybe the opposite was true. She certainly didn't look pregnant yet, so if people didn't know, tongues wouldn't wag. "He didn't attend his other brother's wedding, but he had a lot going on at that time. I'll be asking him. I'm sure if you come, he'll come."

The girl stopped to give her a quick smile and then kept watering the plants.

"I think you were right, what you thought about the orchids. I'm pretty sure I heard somewhere that you shouldn't water them from the top and they prefer to be watered from underneath, not that I know much about these types of plants."

"You could be right. They're more of a tropical plant and not suited to this climate, but my mother likes them. They wouldn't survive if she didn't have this greenhouse, or hothouse—whatever it is." She looked up at Mary Lou. "I suppose you've heard all about me?"

"Well, I am getting married to Jacob and Jacob is Timothy's brother, so the answer is yes. It was difficult for me to come here because you don't know me, but I just wanted you to know that if you ever want or need anybody to talk to, you can talk to me."

Taylor stopped watering the plants and looked at her. "Thank you, that's kind, but I know what advice you'd give me."

Mary Lou sucked in a quick breath of air.

"Don't look so odd. I'm keeping the baby."

"I already guessed that. Is there anything I can do to help you? Anything at all?"

"I don't think so. I'll probably have to give up my studies and reorganize my life."

"Timothy wants to marry you."

Taylor looked at her and burst out laughing. "I know. We have talked about it, but I'm way too young, and I know he wants to go back to the Amish community. And that just wouldn't do, not for me."

"Did he say he wants to come back?"

"You don't know?"

"I haven't talked to Timothy directly. He's not really talking to anybody about it. I know he's talked to Jacob, and maybe one or two of his other brothers."

"I want to thank you for coming here. That was very brave of you."

Mary Lou smiled and considered she'd done the right thing to come. It had been scary, but she'd pushed her nerves aside, and made the effort for the Fuller family and for Timothy's baby.

"Can I give you my address?" Mary Lou asked.

"Yeah, sure. Come into the house. Don't worry, there's no one home. My parents are on vacation. Oh, I think I told you that already. My mind's been fuzzy lately. Anyway, they were so shocked at the news that my mother decided she needed to go on a cruise to recover from the idea of being a granny."

The girl put the watering can down, and Mary Lou

followed her into the house. "Oh! Wow, this is beautiful!" It was all open plan and the ceilings were so high.

"Thank you. Take a seat."

Mary Lou sat down at a large wooden table with bright-floral upholstered high-backed chairs. The material was soft to the touch, like velvet, and they were so different from anything that would ever be seen in an Amish home. "I like these chairs." Mary Lou ran her fingertips over the fabric.

"So does my mother, but they're not my taste. I don't like bright colours." Taylor passed pen and paper to her, and Mary Lou wrote down her address.

Just as Mary Lou finished they heard a knock on the door.

There was a security monitor in the kitchen, and Taylor pointed to it. "Is that one of your Amish friends?"

Mary Lou was furious to see that it was Magnolia. She had told her explicitly to stay outside and not be seen. "I'm so sorry. I told her to wait in the street for me. That's my annoying cousin, Magnolia."

"Magnolia? What a pretty name."

"Don't bother answering the door, I've taken up enough of your time today. I'll write down the time of the wedding, too, just in case you'd like to come." Mary Lou put her head down and jotted the date and time of the wedding. "The wedding's being held at my house."

"Thank you, Mary Lou. I've never been to an Amish

wedding. And I must say that I am curious. I might come."

"Really?"

"Yes. Do I have to tell you now?"

"No. Just show up."

"Don't you need to know the numbers?"

"Not at all. We publish the wedding in the Amish paper and people also come by word-of-mouth. We never know how many are going to show up."

Taylor nodded.

"I hope you do come." Mary Lou stood up and then pushed the chair back under the table. After she'd looked around, she said, "Which way to the front door?"

"Oh, sorry, right this way." Taylor walked Mary Lou to the front door and Mary Lou walked out, saw Magnolia and grabbed her by the arm, pulling her along down the stairs so she wouldn't say anything silly to the girl she had just made friends with. "Come on, Magnolia." She turned around and said goodbye to Taylor when they were a little distance from the house.

Taylor waved and closed the door.

"What happened?" Magnolia asked once they were back at the side of the road.

"What happened was that I told you not to go near the *haus.* What were you thinking?"

Magnolia pouted. "I don't see why I have to be left out of things all the time."

"Because this has nothing to do with you."

"And it also has nothing to do with you. It's between Timothy and that girl."

Magnolia's lips turned down at the corners. "It's their mistake and they have to give account of that on the Day of Judgment."

"It sounds like you're doing a bit of judging yourself, Magnolia."

"I'm not judging anybody."

"I'm annoyed at you for not doing what you were told."

"You can't tell me what to do all the time, Mary Lou. We're both adults, so we're on the same level. Anyway, there was no harm done, was there?"

"None at all. Only because I didn't let you meet her. I have no idea what tactless thing you would've said to her, considering your attitude."

"I wouldn't have said anything about her situation at all. I don't know why you couldn't let me meet her. She seems nice."

"*Jah*, she is nice. And it would be a happy ending if she joined us, got married to Timothy, and had the *boppli* within the community. Timothy could be happy like his older brothers instead of being miserable."

"I guess so."

"What do you mean, you guess so?" Mary Lou held up her hand. "Forget it. Don't say another thing. I don't want to hear what you've got to say."

"Where are we going?" Magnolia said looking

around. "You should've asked that girly if you could call a taxi from her house."

"Girly?"

"Girl."

Mary Lou shook her head. "This is an example of why I didn't want you to meet her. Now, there should be a public phone box around somewhere."

"Well I don't see one."

"We'll just have to walk until we come across a busy road."

"I don't feel like walking too far. These are my new shoes and I haven't walked them in yet."

Mary Lou laughed.

"What's so funny?"

"You just said you 'haven't walked them in yet.'"

"That's right. That's how we say it where I come from. And, anyway, my feet are already tired from walking up and down the street by that girl's house."

Mary Lou shook her head. She couldn't wait to marry Jacob and then she would be in her own house and she could invite only the people she wanted to stay.

"Is she coming to the wedding or what?" Magnolia asked after they had walked a few more paces.

"She said she might."

"That's *wunderbaar* news. Why didn't you tell me first thing?"

"I don't know, but it is good news, isn't it?" Mary Lou felt very good about herself, helping the family she was soon to join. Jacob would be so pleased, and more than anything she wanted his approval.

"It is."

"Now we only have to hope that Timothy can come to the wedding as well."

"Isn't he coming?"

Mary Lou shrugged her shoulders. "I'm not sure. Jacob told him he's welcome. We'll just have to wait and see."

CHAPTER 2

AFTER MARY LOU and Magnolia had walked for half an hour, Mary Lou admitted they were not going to find a public phone box. They finally encountered a man riding a bike and Mary Lou flagged him down. He was around thirty and looked as though he was a professional bike rider in his gaudy head-to-toe lycra suit.

"Stop it, Mary Lou. What are you doing?"

Magnolia had grabbed onto Mary Lou's sleeve and Mary Lou pulled her arm away from her cousin's grasp. "Excuse me," she said to the bike rider, "Would you have a cell phone?"

He looked them up and down, apparently missing the irony as his expression revealed how odd-looking he found their traditional Amish clothing. "I do."

"We're stuck here and we were wondering if you might be able to call us a taxi?"

"Sure." The man ripped his cell phone from the

Velcro band around his arm and called for a taxi. "Done," he said with a big smile as he reattached his phone.

"Thank you," Mary Lou said.

"You're welcome. Bye."

"What do we do now?" Magnolia asked when the man had ridden away.

"Wait right here, of course. Why do you always second-guess everything I do? You were trying to stop me from talking to that man just now."

"I didn't know what you were doing."

"You're younger than me, and less experienced. You must just trust me. I know what I'm doing."

"Okay, I'll try."

"Good."

They leaned against a fence until the taxi pulled up ten minutes later. Mary Lou's feet were sore, although she'd no intention of admitting it to Magnolia, and the approaching taxi was one of the best sights she'd seen in a long time.

"My feet are aching," said Magnolia when she got into the taxi.

Mary Lou's resolve wavered, and she replied, "So are mine."

"I've got the new shoes, though."

"Not everything has to be a competition."

"It's not a competition. It's just that my feet are sore."

"Excuse me, ladies. Where are we going?" the driver

asked.

Mary Lou gave him the address of the diner by the park.

As they slid into the only booth left unoccupied, Mary Lou reminded herself yet again to make a real effort to be nice to Magnolia. "Things happened last time you were here, Magnolia, and I'm prepared to forget them and move on."

"You're saying that as though I've done something wrong."

"It's just not good to talk about it. No one was right and no one was wrong. Let's leave things like that."

"Okay." Magnolia picked up the menu and studied it and then put it back down on the table. "I have to say something about last time I was here."

"Go ahead."

"I have to tell you that I'm annoyed that you told me the only boy in the community I couldn't have was Jacob Fuller. What you didn't say was that you liked him, and we had agreed to tell each other everything."

"It was a complicated thing. I liked him, but I didn't think he'd ever like me." And, she'd liked each of his three older brothers, too, but she didn't want to think about that or bring it up to Magnolia.

"And you certainly didn't think that he'd like me," Magnolia said.

"Yes, that's right."

"Well, you must think I'm badly unattractive."

"I don't. I don't at all." She saw her cousin's sad face. "You'll find someone, don't worry."

"Will you help me, Mary Lou?" Magnolia lunged forward and grabbed Mary Lou's arm.

Mary Lou looked down at her arm. She wanted to concentrate on her wedding, at this most-exciting time in her life, not try to find her hard-to-please cousin a boyfriend and possibly a husband. "It's just that it's the worst time ever for me to do something like that. How about next time you come and visit?" So that Magnolia wouldn't think she could stay at her house when that next time came, she added, "The next time you come and stay at *Mamm's*."

"I don't know when that will be and I'll be so much older. My chances will be lessened."

After the waitress had come and taken their food and drink order, Mary Lou had a good think about what Magnolia had said. She was right about her chances being fewer with each passing year. All the suitable men tended to get married very young, before they were even twenty sometimes. Reminding herself that she was turning over a new leaf, she said, "Okay I'll help you."

"Do you mean it?"

"If I said it, I mean it."

"Oh, *denke*, Mary Lou." Magnolia scratched her square chin. "What about one of the other Fuller boys? There are three of them left."

Mary Lou shrugged her shoulders. "You got along with Samuel last time you were here."

"I did, didn't I?"

"Jah, so what do you think of him?"

"I don't know. Is there anyone else you can think of?"

"Timothy is out because … well, you know. Then there's Benjamin who's too young, way too young."

"Benjamin's personality doesn't suit mine anyway."

"That's true. He's not a very serious person, whereas Samuel is."

"I don't know. I don't have to date one of the Fullers."

Mary Lou was tempted to point out she probably couldn't even get Samuel and that beggars couldn't be choosers. The only reason Samuel hadn't married and didn't even have a girlfriend was that he was painfully shy and way too quiet. It was hard being tactful and good-natured. It was a lot of work, but Mary Lou was determined to be that better person that Jacob and his family deserved. And if that meant finding a husband for her dull cousin instead of fully enjoying her wedding preparations and proceedings, then that was exactly what she would do. "I don't know what to do with you, Magnolia."

"What do you mean?"

Mary Lou didn't answer her question, as the waitress arrived and began arranging their food on the table.

"Thank you," Mary Lou said to her before she left, receiving a nod of acknowledgement.

"Yes, thank you," Magnolia parroted.

Mary Lou stared at her cousin. "You can't get a better man than Samuel."

"I don't know if I'm in love with him."

Mary Lou looked down at her food. "I suppose that's just as well." She picked up her corned beef and pickle sandwich and bit into it.

"What do you mean?" Magnolia asked.

She finished chewing, and then said, "It's just as well you don't like Samuel because that would have been a real problem for me."

Magnolia narrowed her eyes. "Why would it be a problem to you?"

"Because... do you remember my good friends Lucy and Adeline? They married two of Jacob's brothers."

"*Jah*, I know Lucy and Adeline."

"They have a younger *schweschder*, Catherine."

"I know Catherine, too."

"Catherine would be very disappointed if you liked Samuel."

Mary Lou watched Magnolia's gaze drop to the plate of food in front of her. A little bit of competition, even if it was imagined, was a healthy thing in Mary Lou's mind. And Mary Lou knew what a competitive person her cousin was. Magnolia wouldn't find a better man than Samuel to marry, so Mary Lou excused herself for the small deception. Mary Lou didn't know what Catherine thought of Samuel.

Magnolia looked back up at Mary Lou. "She really likes him?"

"The three Miller girls marrying three of the Fuller boys. Don't you think that would be so perfect and cute?"

"*Nee!* I don't! I don't at all. We did get along well when I was here last time."

"*Jah,* and he talked to you for a long time and he hardly talks to anyone."

"I think I might like him."

Shaking her head, Mary Lou said, "That's a problem." Mary Lou was pleased her plan was working exactly as she planned.

"I think I should get to know him a little better. He can make his choice who he likes. Do you still want to help me, Mary Lou?"

"*Jah.* I'll help you. We might pay the Fullers a little visit today."

"Will they be home?" Magnolia asked.

"They'll be home after work. Now, eat up your food. We'll get a taxi home and then we'll hitch the buggy and take a drive out to the Fullers.'"

"*Denke,* Mary Lou. I'm so grateful to have a cousin like you."

"I'm telling you this now, not many women would take on the burden of finding you a husband just before they get married. It's going to be a lot of work, but that's just what sort of person I am."

Magnolia looked thoughtful and bit into her sandwich.

AFTER FIVE O'CLOCK they arrived at the Fullers.' Mrs. Fuller was delighted to see them and ushered them into the kitchen for milk and cookies.

"We won't stay long, Mrs. Fuller," Mary Lou said. "I just want a quick word with Jacob."

"That's fine. Stay for the evening meal if you'd like."

"Thanks, but my folks are expecting us home."

They sat and ate cookies while Mrs. Fuller completed her preparations for the meal.

"Is there anything I can do to help?"

"*Nee,* Mary Lou. I'm about done."

"It smells very nice," Magnolia said.

"It's just a beef pie. Nothing too special."

"Mrs. Fuller's a really good cook."

Just as Mrs. Fuller laughed they heard a buggy. When Mrs. Fuller heard it too, she peered out the window. "That's them now."

Mary Lou half stood and looked out the window. She saw Benjamin, Jacob, and Mr. Fuller get out of the buggy, but not Samuel.

"We'll go now." Mary Lou stood up and pushed her chair back in under the table.

"Okay. It was nice to see both of you."

Magnolia looked confused, but got up from her chair too.

Mrs. Miller walked them to the door and then Mary Lou excused herself from the two ladies and pulled Jacob aside. "Where's Samuel?"

He frowned at her and then gave her a crooked smile. "Hello."

She smiled back and felt a little guilty. "Hello."

"It's nice to see you too." His lips turned upward.

"Where's Samuel?" she asked again.

"He's having dinner at Isaac's tonight."

"Oh."

He glanced over her shoulder at Magnolia. "Doing a little matchmaking?"

"Shh. Don't you say anything to anyone."

He chuckled. "I won't."

"Well, we should go."

"So quick? I've hardly had time to say two words to you. Meet me tomorrow at lunchtime?"

"What for?"

"Lunch, of course."

"Oh." Mary Lou laughed. "I'd like that."

"Meet me at the usual place?"

"I finish at one tomorrow. I thought I'd finish early and spend some time with Magnolia before the wedding."

He pulled a sad face. "What about me? Why don't we meet just after one and we can have a quick lunch before you go home?"

She could never say no to him. "Okay. I'll go there as soon as I finish work. Then I'll go home afterward."

"Good."

They exchanged smiles and couldn't even give each other a quick kiss because Magnolia and Mrs. Fuller were watching them from the porch.

Mary Lou waved Magnolia over and said goodbye to Mrs. Fuller. Mrs. Fuller waited on the porch with Jacob until they drove the buggy away.

"Well, where is he?" Magnolia asked.

"Having dinner at Isaac's."

Magnolia slumped into the seat and Mary Lou said, "Cheer up. I'm finishing early tomorrow so I can spend some time with you."

"Really?"

"*Jah.*"

"I should be home at two, or two thirty."

"What can we do?"

"Anything you like." Mary Lou saw a little smile on her cousin's lips.

"Anything at all?"

"*Jah.*"

CHAPTER 3

Mary Lou was running a little late and when she got to the café where she had arranged to meet Jacob, he was sitting there with white paper bags in his hands. He jumped up when he saw her.

"There's been a change of plans. Timothy needs to speak to me urgently." He passed her a bag. "We're having take-out. Do you mind?"

"*Nee,* of course not. Is he okay?"

"We'll need to hurry." On the way out, he explained that she'd have to wait in the buggy while he talked to Timothy at the park where the brothers had arranged to meet. "It's just that he might not speak what's on his mind if you're there."

"I totally understand." It was to have been the alone time she'd been hoping for, but family came first.

They pulled up at the park and then Mary Lou spotted Timothy in the distance. "Here he comes. He'll feel awkward if he knows I'm here too. Just don't tell him I'm here. Go and sit on that bench and wait for him and I'll stay here and eat."

"Are you sure?"

"Jah. He won't be able to see me if you sit there."

"Denke, Mary Lou, for being so understanding." He leaned over and gave her a tiny kiss on her cheek and then jumped out of the buggy.

The park seat was only a little distance behind the buggy and when Timothy arrived, Mary Lou discovered it was close enough for her to overhear what was said.

After Timothy had greeted his brother, he said, "Things have always worked out well for you, Jacob,"

"That's true, they have."

She peeped out at the two of them, being careful that Timothy didn't see her.

Timothy rubbed his forehead and she could see his frustration. It was written over his entire body. "I wish I was more like you. I've made a real mess of my life."

"Nee, you haven't."

"I have, it's true. Having a baby out of wedlock with an *Englisch* girl isn't the best start to life, especially with her not wanting to marry me. She could take the baby anywhere, and I'll never see either of them again."

"You must pray and put the matter into *Gott's* hands. That's all you can do."

Timothy rubbed his stubbly chin. He looked like he hadn't slept for four days and hadn't shaved for three.

"I hesitate to do that," Timothy said.

"Why's that?"

"What if it's *Gott's* will that I never see the *boppli?*"

Jacob shook his head. "I can't answer that."

"Well, it might be, mightn't it? I made stupid mistakes and now maybe I'm being punished."

"Everyone makes mistakes and everyone sins. There's not one who hasn't. You must ask forgiveness."

"So, what you're saying is that I need to come back to the community? I thought about doing that, but that might drive Taylor even further away from me. I'm sure it would. That's why I can't." Timothy swallowed hard.

Mary Lou knew how he would've felt with three of his older brothers married, and soon Jacob would marry her. They'd all married Amish girls, and he'd gotten involved with an *Englisch* girl and disappointed their parents.

Jacob said, "I can't tell you what to do. You must make your own decisions about things."

"What would you do?"

"I can't say, because I don't know what I would do in your situation. I think I would return to the community, hope and pray. That's all you can do."

"I'll think about coming back, I will."

"You said you were coming back anyway —eventually."

"I never meant to stay away forever, but things have changed. I was just going on *rumspringa* for a year or two, like everyone else does. I just wanted to experience life on the outside for a bit. Something like this happening never entered my dumb head."

"I'm sure you're not the only one who's had problems like this. Perhaps you should talk to the bishop?"

Timothy sighed. "I don't know. Things have a sense of finality to them if I go to the bishop. If he advises me to return and I don't, I just feel I'll fall further away from things."

"He agrees with the young going on *rumspringa,* so they can fully commit to the community and get baptized on their return."

"I know."

"He might give you some good advice."

"That's one of the things I'm afraid of. What if he does, but I don't want to take it?"

Mary Lou could feel Timothy's pain. She knew he wouldn't like to be burdening Jacob right now, so close before the wedding.

"I suppose *Mamm* is happy about you marrying Mary Lou?"

Mary Lou's heart pumped hard as she listened to Jacob's answer.

"She's delighted. She's always liked Mary Lou, that's what she said. I don't think she did at the very start though, but she does now."

"You mean when she was first dating Isaac?"

"That's right. I think it takes *Mamm* a while to warm to people. I'm not sure why."

Timothy chuckled. "I guess that's true. And how is the business doing?"

"It's doing well and there's a place for you whenever you come back."

"Thanks. I'll be back, hopefully, some time." Timothy had worked at the family joinery business and had left when he moved out of the family home to go on *rumspringa*. He'd told his father he needed some separation from the family and he'd gotten a job elsewhere.

"*Mamm* and *Dat* think I've brought shame upon them."

"Well, we shall see. The news will be out soon. News always travels pretty fast in the community."

"I could've done with time away from everyone, so I can make a clear-headed decision. That's not likely to happen, not with the long hours of my two jobs. I need all the money to pay the rent now that my two house-mates have moved on."

"Can't you find other people to move in?"

"No. That could bring me more problems. Along with paying the rent, I'm still paying back money for that second car I managed to crash. With no insurance, I'm still paying back the loan I took out to buy it. Now I walk everywhere or catch buses."

Mary Lou remembered he had bought a car outright with a friend of his and had crashed it. It was news to her that he'd had an accident in the second one also.

"Do you need money? I can give you some."

Mary Lou's ears pricked. They needed that money for their house and their life together. Then she relaxed. Timothy was part of their family and if he needed help, that was fine.

"Thanks, but I don't like taking money. I would if I was starving but I'm not there yet. I feel like I'm drowning in debt and that makes me even more unattractive to Taylor. How can I support a wife and child if I can't support myself?"

"You look miserable. Why don't you do something nice for the rest of the day?"

"On Saturday afternoons, I usually do something with my friends, but today I just want to be on my own. It's a rare day that I'm not working."

"Have you prayed about your situation?"

"I do want *Gott* to help me. Only thing is, what if He doesn't want the same outcome as I want? If Taylor's not meant to be one of our community—if it's not in *Gott's* will, I could pray until I'm blue in the face and it won't happen."

"Where's Taylor at with everything?"

Timothy shook his head. "There's no use talking to Taylor. She told me she just needs space."

"Are you coming to my wedding?" Jacob asked.

"I intend to, unless something unexpected turns up. I feel awful for missing Joshua's, but it coincided with the dramas I was having."

"I know, and he understands."

Timothy stood. "I should go."

"I hope I'll see you at the wedding. Mary Lou would really like you to be there as well."

He shrugged his shoulders. "Don't worry, I'll do my best to be there."

"I hope so. It wouldn't be the same without all my family there."

"It'll mean I'll have to see *Mamm* and *Dat* again. Remember how she was the day I told them the news?" Timothy grunted. "I haven't seen them since."

Jacob stood up and slapped him on his shoulder. "I might see you, then."

Timothy gave Jacob a smile and hit him on the shoulder. Then Jacob playfully swiped at him and Timothy ducked away. The two of them laughed and said goodbye to one another.

As Timothy walked away, Jacob watched him for a little while and then got back into the buggy next to Mary Lou.

"What happened?" she asked as though she hadn't been able to hear the whole thing.

"He said he might come to the wedding. I guess he doesn't know what Taylor is doing. Up until he met her, he didn't have a care in the world. He's really suffering." Jacob put his arm around Mary Lou. "We've been blessed with what we have. Love is a painful experience for him."

"I know. It would've been so much easier if he'd fallen in love with an Amish girl."

"That would've been better. *Mamm's* dreadfully upset," Jacob said as he pulled the buggy onto the road.

"I can imagine."

"She said that things like that just don't happen in our family."

"She was right, they hadn't happened, not until now."

"I have to go back to work."

"Take me back to my buggy first. Then I'm going home to do something with Magnolia. I promised her we'd do something together this afternoon."

"That's nice."

"Hmm. I don't know; it depends what she wants to do. She's telling me when I get there."

Jacob tossed his head back and laughed. "It could be anything, knowing that it's Magnolia."

"I know." She looked at him with a wry grin, and laughed along.

MARY LOU WALKED into her home, and there was Magnolia waiting for her, looking bright and fresh faced.

"There you are," Magnolia said.

"I came as fast as I could."

"You said we can do anything I choose, right?"

"*Jah*, within reason. We can't go to the moon or Mars."

"What about to Catherine's place?"

Mary Lou was taken aback. It would be dreadful if Magnolia found out she had made the whole thing up about Catherine liking Samuel. She couldn't think of a good excuse not to go, though, so she had to agree. "All right if that's where you want to go."

"Good. Shall we leave now? It's already late."

"Okay, I'll just tell *Mamm* where we're going."

"No need. I've already told her." Magnolia all but pushed Mary Lou out the door.

On their way to the Millers' *haus,* Mary Lou asked, "Why do you want to see Catherine?"

"I want to visit Catherine to see what she says. If they aren't properly together yet, I'll know I still have time."

Mary Lou sighed. That was her worst fear. All of a sudden it hit her; did she really want Magnolia as a sister-in-law? "Okay."

CHAPTER 4

CATHERINE MILLER WAS QUIETLY SEWING her quilt while she was alone at home. More than anything, she wanted to get married and she was sewing the quilt to add to her hope chest. With each small stitch she hand-sewed, she thought about the life she'd have with her perfect man, whoever he was, and the happy home they'd share. One day that quilt would adorn her marriage bed. She was waiting on *Gott* to let her know whom He wanted her to marry. If *Gott* chose her husband, then no mistake could be made. She didn't want to spend her life in regret, and the Amish married for life.

Her two older sisters had married two of the Fuller boys and they were happy. Catherine wanted to be just like them. Neither of them had children yet, and maybe if she married soon all their children could grow up close in age. In Catherine's mind, that was a perfect scenario.

She often thought about her day—her wedding day. There would be hundreds of guests who would come to watch her and her husband get married. And then they would have a magnificent wedding feast at her parents' home. Ideally, her husband would be handsome and taller than she. He would be confident, and good-natured. He would be firm but fair with their many children and he would enjoy spending time with them and with her.

She looked out the window feeling lonely and little bit blue. It was certainly quiet now that she was the only child left at home. She didn't want to visit her sisters too often now that they were married, especially not on a Saturday when their husbands would be at home. She knew the Fullers' joinery factory rarely opened on a Saturday unless they were busy with orders.

When she heard a buggy, she was curious. She knew it wouldn't be her parents as they'd only just left. She threaded the needle into the material, placed it all on the couch beside her, got up and ran to see who it was. She was delighted to see that it was Mary Lou and, looking harder, it seemed to be her cousin beside her.

She swung the door open and walked out to meet them.

The girls greeted each other and when Mary Lou

stepped down from the buggy, Catherine helped to secure it.

"Come inside. Would you like lemonade and cookies?"

"We'd love some," Magnolia said.

They followed Catherine inside and sat down at the kitchen table. As Catherine got the lemonade and cookies organized she said, "I'm so pleased you came to visit me. I'm lonely here now that my sisters have married."

"Mary Lou took some time off and I thought it would be nice to see you."

"I'm glad you did. How are all the wedding preparations, Mary Lou?"

"Everything's under control. The dresses and suits are finished and we're starting on the food."

"Can I do anything?"

"Not at this stage, but I will let you know if you can soon. I'll ask *Mamm* what you can do. Thanks for offering."

"I'd love to help. And how long are you staying here for this time, Magnolia?"

"I'm not sure yet. Mary Lou's *mudder* said I could stay as long as I like."

"You like this community?" Catherine asked as she sat and poured the lemonade and passed them each a glass.

"*Jah*, it's fine. I do like it." Magnolia took a sip of

lemonade, and then blurted out, "Catherine, what do you think of Samuel?"

Catherine tilted her head, thinking it was quite odd to ask something like that right out of left field. "Do you mean Samuel Fuller?" She pushed the plate of cookies toward them and each girl took one.

"*Jah.*"

"He's nice."

Magnolia took another sip of lemonade and looked at Mary Lou, who looked extremely uncomfortable. It made no sense to Catherine when she saw the way the cousins looked at one another.

"Are you okay, Mary Lou?"

"*Jah*, just wedding nerves, I guess, bride-to-be nerves." Mary Lou giggled.

"You must be so happy."

"I am, very happy."

Magnolia interrupted, "So you don't think Samuel is too quiet?" She stared directly at Catherine.

Catherine looked startled at Magnolia's butting in. "Well, he is quiet, but I think that's just his personality. He's never been rude or anything."

"When do you think you'll get married, Catherine?" Magnolia asked.

"Me?" Catherine felt a little disoriented by Magnolia's disconnected questions.

Magnolia nodded, and Catherine giggled as she said, "I don't know."

"So, no one's asked you?"

"*Nee.* I haven't even gone on a buggy ride with anyone yet."

Mary Lou blurted out, "This is such a nice version of lemonade, Catherine."

"Do you think so?"

"I do." Mary Lou took another sip.

"It has extra lemons in it and less sugar than some people think it should have, but my family really likes it like this."

Mary Lou picked up a cookie. "Did you make these, Catherine?"

"*Jah,* I love to make cookies and cakes. If I'd known you were coming I would've baked cupcakes. I love piping the frosting into a whirl on top."

"Frosting is definitely the best part," Magnolia said.

Catherine looked over at Magnolia. "I think so too."

"It seems we have the same taste in everything, Catherine."

"Is that right? What things do we both like?"

Right at that moment, Mary Lou spilled her drink all over the table. "Oh! Look what I've done. I'm so clumsy sometimes."

"No harm done. Unless you got some on your dress?"

"*Nee,* I didn't."

Catherine got a tea towel from beside the sink and mopped up all the spilled lemonade. Meanwhile, she caught Mary Lou glaring at Magnolia. Catherine couldn't work that out because Mary Lou was the one who'd spilled the lemonade, not Magnolia.

"We should really get going anyway. I'm sorry to be so clumsy. Will you forgive me?"

"Of course," said Catherine. "An accident like that could happen to anyone."

"Come on, Magnolia. We really should get going."

Magnolia took another cookie. "Do we have to? We only just got here."

"*Jah*, we should get home to help with the evening meal."

Magnolia bit into the cookie and then stood up. "*Denke* for the lemonade and the cookies, Catherine."

"You're welcome. Stay longer next time."

"We will," Mary Lou said as she almost pushed Magnolia toward the front door.

"Can I have another cookie?" Magnolia asked.

"Sure." Catherine picked up the plate and offered it to her, and Magnolia took two more cookies. "Mary Lou?" Catherine asked.

"*Nee denke.*"

Catherine watched from the porch as they both climbed into the buggy. Magnolia was still chomping on cookies, and Mary Lou looked most distressed. It seemed odd that they'd come for such a quick visit.

She hadn't said anything to offend them, but she'd often been accused of being too frank, and speaking her mind when she should've remained silent. Catherine went back inside to clean up the kitchen. As she was putting the remaining cookies back in the jar, it came to her in a flash that she'd been praying for God to show her a good man and then Samuel's name kept coming up in the conversation.

Could this have been *Gott's* way of bringing Samuel to her attention? She'd always overlooked him because he was quiet and she wanted someone confident and more outspoken. Maybe he was the perfect man for her and he'd been under her nose that whole time. Then it occurred to her that everyone told her she was confident and outspoken, so maybe it could be a case of opposites attracting, or of opposites balancing each other.

"It's Samuel," she said to herself. "That makes sense now. *Denke, Gott,* for showing me that Samuel Fuller is the man I should marry." She remembered how in the bible God spoke to Balaam through a donkey. It was recorded in Numbers 22, and just like it happened in that story, the two girls had come directly with a message for her. "They probably had no idea why they came here. *Gott* had his hand on them for my sake."

While Catherine washed up the dishes, she couldn't help giggling as she thought of Mary Lou and Magnolia being like two donkeys. Then she told herself she was being mean, so she stopped laughing. Once the kitchen was clean, she sat down and continued sewing her quilt. But now she knew she was sewing it for her and Samuel.

~

WHEN MARY LOU got down to the end of the driveway, she had finally calmed down enough to speak to her cousin. "What was all that about in there?"

"I don't know what you're talking about." Crumbs flew out of Magnolia's mouth as she spoke.

Mary Lou had to look away. "You questioned her about Samuel."

"Did I?"

"*Jah.* That's why I had to spill the lemonade."

"You did that deliberately?"

"I had to. You forced me to do it."

"Mary Lou, I did nothing of the kind."

"Not literally, but if I hadn't then she would know that you like Samuel as well and don't you think that would have made for an awkward situation?" Mary Lou was upset that her harmless lie to get Magnolia to like Samuel had nearly been found out.

"You said she likes him, so I just wondered how far things have gotten between them."

"What does it matter? They're not official, are they? Otherwise, everybody would know."

"You know about them."

"I'm good friends with her two sisters. Anyway, let's talk about something else."

Magnolia grunted. "Like what?"

"Like where you'd like to go now."

"You said we had to go back home."

"I suppose we should. We need to make enough food for tonight, and for tomorrow, too, seeing it's Sunday."

"I'll help."

"*Denke.*"

"Who's *haus* will the meeting be at tomorrow?"

"It's going to be at the bishop's *haus.*"

"Oh, I was hoping it might be at the Fullers.' How are you going to help me with Samuel?"

Mary Lou couldn't help smiling. "You're openly admitting to liking him now?"

"*Jah,* I do. I always have liked him and I think he likes me too. We've had many good conversations."

"*Jah,* I think the two of you would be good together."

"How are you going to make it happen?"

"You'll have to do some of the work. It can't be all up to me, you know."

Magnolia nodded. "I know that. Of course, I do. I'll do whatever you say."

"Good. I'll think of something. I'll think of some way of having the two of you together somewhere."

Magnolia slumped back into the buggy seat and continued nibbling on her cookie.

CHAPTER 5

CATHERINE WAS PLEASED to sit with her sisters at the meeting. It was often the only time she saw them these days. With the meetings having the men on one side and the women on the other, Catherine had them away from their husbands and that meant she had their attention for a few minutes before the meeting started. When the meeting was over, her two older sisters joined their husbands and Catherine was back to being alone. Sure, she had her friends, but it wasn't the same.

She took a plate and helped herself to the food on the long table. Then she looked around for a friend to sit with. She spotted Samuel Fuller eating by himself, and she made her way over to him. She'd always preferred that the man would be the one to make the first move, and that's how she'd always pictured things when they played out in her mind, but she reminded herself of the scripture that said faith without works is dead. If she expected *Gott* to provide her with a husband, she had to add some form of action with her faith.

"Hi, Samuel, mind if I sit down?"

"Sure." He offered a huge smile. "I mean, no. I don't mind. That's sort of a backwards question. Please join me."

She sat and started eating, not knowing what to say. They'd been together at family gatherings, since her two sisters had married two of his brothers, but they'd never talked much. Normally, she wasn't shy but now that Magnolia had started her thinking about getting married, she was nervous speaking to him.

"Have you been doing anything for Jacob's wedding?" Catherine asked.

"Nee, there's not much to do."

That much was true. There was a lot more for the bride's family since they normally made the suits and the dresses, and they made the food, and the wedding was almost always held at the bride's family's home. "How's work?" she asked.

"Pretty good."

She looked down at her food. He was making conversation very difficult.

"And what do you do with yourself these days?"

At last. She looked across at him and smiled. "I don't have a job or anything, but I've been thinking about getting one. It's awfully lonely at home with my sisters both gone now."

"*Jah,* I know what you mean. Once Jacob gets married it'll only be me and Benjamin."

"That's right, because Timothy's still on *rumspringa.*"

"I don't know if he'll come back. He's having a hard time of it."

"Why's that?"

He shook his head. "It's just he's having personal issues."

Catherine leaned forward and whispered, "Is it a woman?"

"What have you heard?"

She straightened up. "Nothing."

He chuckled. "*Jah,* it's a woman. He's had other problems, but the woman is the main one."

"I hope everything turns out all right for him."

"*Denke.* I'm sure it will. We're all praying for him."

"I will too, then."

"Would you?"

"*Jah,* of course. I don't have to know about what's going on if you don't want to tell me. *Gott* knows what's happening."

"I'd appreciate the prayer. *Denke.*"

She kept eating, hoping he'd ask her out. He continued to eat in silence.

SAMUEL LOOKED down at his food and wanted to kick himself hard. Why was talking to women so easy for his brothers? Catherine was the one girl he liked and now that she was in front of him, he could barely say two words. What he wanted to do was ask her on a picnic, but what if she said no? He'd feel dreadful. He searched his mind for a question. If he could keep her talking, that might make her like him. "What kind of job would you do if you could do anything?"

Her eyes sparkled. "I think I'd like to have a quilt store one day. I love quilts. I've always loved sewing."

"That's interesting. Have you sewn many quilts?"

"I've worked on some with *Mamm,* and I'm working on one by myself right now. I'll have it finished in ... Honestly, I'm not sure when I'll have it finished. I'm doing it all by hand instead of with a machine."

"Why's that? *Mamm's* got a gas-powered sewing machine and she loves it."

"I think it's because I like to put thought into my stitches. It's not so much sewing it to get it finished, it's sewing it because I love sewing it."

"I see. You want to go slow?"

She laughed. "It sounds like madness, I know."

"Nee, it doesn't. It sounds just *wunderbaar."* He was falling more in love with her the more he spoke to her. Most women would sew a thing aiming to get it finished. How unique to sew just for the passion of the sewing itself. He was pleased with himself for asking a good question. He was getting to know a lot more about her.

"What do you like to do?"

"I like working with wood, which is good because that's what I spend most of the day doing."

"I know your firm makes kitchen cabinets mostly, but what part of it do you do?"

"It's not too exciting, really, just cutting the doors to shape and putting on the hinges. It's a production line. There's nothing very creative about it. Not the part I do."

"You like to be creative?"

"*Jah*, I do."

"With wood?"

"*Jah*. It's in the blood, I guess. Going back generations we've all been good with our hands—working with wood." He stared into her eyes. No one had ever bothered to ask what he liked to do. "That's what I do when I'm not working. I make things. I usually make little things for *Mamm* for her kitchen—spoons, pot holders, jam pots, salt and pepper shakers."

"Did you make the tall ones that are in the center of her dining table?"

"*Jah*, I did. I made them when I was about seventeen."

"They're lovely."

"*Denke.*"

CHAPTER 6

JUST AFTER THE post-service meal had started, Mary Lou looked around for Samuel, so she could send Magnolia over. When she saw him, she was upset to see that Catherine was talking to him. They were sitting at a table in the back of the yard and, even worse, they were by themselves.

Magnolia hadn't seen the two of them together yet because she was speaking to one of the older ladies who was asking about her mother. Different scenarios ran through Mary Lou's head as she wondered the best way to handle the situation. What if it were true and Catherine did like him? That was something she hadn't figured on.

Mrs. Fuller walked up to her. "I suppose you heard about what happened with Timothy?" Mrs. Fuller asked her right out of the blue.

"*Jah*. I heard."

"It's only right that Jacob told you. It's just so awful."

"I met Taylor and she seems nice."

Mrs. Fuller stared at her in horror. "Where did you meet her?"

Mary Lou didn't want her future mother-in-law to think she was meddling. "I was in town one time with Jacob and he pointed her out." That was close to the truth. It would've been more comfortable to lie about the rest, but she couldn't bring herself to do so. This new leaf she had turned over was often inconvenient. "I found out where she lived and I went there."

Mrs. Fuller's jaw dropped. "Why ever would you do something like that?"

"I just wanted to help."

"What did she say?"

Mary Lou shrugged. She hadn't planned to let anyone know she'd even talked to Taylor. "I asked her to my wedding. She said she might come."

"Oh, Mary Lou, do you think there might be any chance she'd join us?"

Mary Lou hated to crush Mrs. Fuller's hopes. It was rare that anyone ever joined the Amish and a great percentage of the fraction who did, didn't last long. "I really don't know."

"Did she say anything else?"

"Not really. She just talked about plants."

"Really? She keeps vegetables?"

"Flowers, orchids they were, and I think they were her mother's. Not much was said. I hope you don't mind me reaching out to her. I thought she might like to talk to a woman, one who's been in the community and out of it." Mary Lou had also been shunned at one time, but there was no need to remind Mrs. Fuller of that whole business.

"That's quite all right, Mary Lou. You have great compassion for people. You will be a blessing to the whole family."

Her words pleased Mary Lou greatly. *"Denke.* I hope so."

"There's no doubt in my mind. Oh, I do hope things work out for Timothy. Now you've given me a glimmer of hope." She smiled at Mary Lou and clasped her hand.

Mary Lou opened her mouth to speak and then closed it. She desperately wanted to tell her not to get her hopes up, but on the other hand, everyone needed hope.

"Mrs. Fuller, how are you?"

Mary Lou hadn't noticed Magnolia walking up alongside Mrs. Fuller until her squawky voice had jolted her, and it must have jolted Mrs. Fuller too, going by her twisted lips.

Mrs. Fuller let go of Mary Lou's hand as she turned to talk to Magnolia. "Oh, hello."

"Mrs. Fuller, you remember my cousin, Magnolia?"

"Of course I do. You've come to help with the wedding, Magnolia?"

"*Jah*, I love to help out and Mary Lou and I have always been close."

"That's good. If you two girls will excuse me, please, I need to talk with the bishop."

Magnolia's mouth turned down at the corners. "Why did she leave so soon, Mary Lou? She seemed pleased to see me."

"She had to speak with the bishop."

"That's what she said, but did she really?"

"I guess."

"What were you talking to her about? Did you put a good word in for me?"

"*Nee*, it wasn't about you. I told her I went to see Taylor."

Magnolia gasped. "Was she upset?"

"She was happy. I just don't want her to get her hopes up too high. All Taylor said was that she might come to the wedding and it's a huge leap from attending an Amish wedding to joining the community."

"*Jah*, that's true. When are you going to match me with him?" Magnolia nodded her head to Samuel. "He's alone now."

"I know."

"He was talking to Catherine before, so you had better move fast. I don't want to miss out. Do you have a plan? I hope you're taking this seriously."

"Not yet ... about the plan, and I am taking it seriously. I'm still thinking on it."

"You'd better hurry."

"I can't work under pressure."

"Just take me over there before he starts talking to someone else, would you?"

~

CATHERINE WALKED AWAY FROM SAMUEL. She'd broken the ice. She wanted to confide in her sisters, but they were talking to other people. Her friend, Nella, was alone, so she headed over to talk with her about Samuel.

"*Jah,* I can see the two of you together," Nella said when Catherine told her how she felt about him.

"Really?" Catherine glanced back at Samuel and saw him still by himself.

"You're outgoing, and he's shy. The two of you would complement one another."

"I guess you're right."

"When did you start liking him?"

"It was a funny thing. I was praying for a man to come into my life and then Mary Lou visited with her cousin and they mentioned him a couple times and then left quickly. And then it occurred to me shortly after they left that maybe he would be a good match. I never really talk to him much, but he's really nice." Catherine swallowed hard. She didn't just think he was nice, she could feel herself falling in love with him.

That was something she didn't want to share with her friend, not just yet.

"Does he know you like him?"

"*Nee,* I don't think so. We just had a nice talk and I'll just wait and see what develops from there."

"Good idea."

Nella was already dating Peter, one of the Fuller boys' cousins.

CHAPTER 7

AFTER SAMUEL LIFTED the last forkful of food from his plate into his mouth, he looked up to see Mary Lou and her cousin, Magnolia, heading toward him. Both had their eyes fixed upon him and he wondered what they wanted. He fixed a smile on his face and hoped Mary Lou wasn't trying to match him with her cousin.

"Hi, Samuel, mind if we sit with you?"

He wiped his mouth with a paper napkin as they both sat down on the other side of the table to face him directly. "Go ahead." By the time he spoke they were already seated. "It's nice to see you again, Magnolia."

"*Denke.* It's nice to see you as well."

She'd given him a sickly smile and then he knew she liked him. He turned his attention to Mary Lou. "Is everything on track for the wedding?"

"*Jah.* All's fine. Everything's already finished except

for the food and that can't be done til the day or a couple of days before. We have a lot of cake."

Magnolia giggled. "Mary Lou loves cake. She has a sweet tooth, just like me."

He didn't know what to do now that he knew Magnolia liked him. The only girl he liked was Catherine. He glanced over the top of their heads looking to see where Catherine had gone. It would be awful if she saw him talking to any other girl. Thankfully, he saw she was deeply engrossed in a conversation with Nella.

Magnolia cleared her throat loudly until Samuel looked back at her. "Until the wedding, I have free time since Mary Lou has done everything. And she's also going to work right up until the wedding and that'll leave me at home, alone."

"What about Mary Lou's *mudder?*" Samuel asked.

"What about her?" Magnolia asked.

"Won't she be keeping you company?"

Slowly, Magnolia nodded. "I guess so, but I was hoping to do something a little more exciting and get out of the *haus.* Maybe get to see more of the countryside."

She was giving him large and obvious hints that she wanted him to show her around. "I'm sure Mary Lou could find someone to show you around, couldn't you, Mary Lou? I'll be working for the next few days, right through until the wedding."

"Still, you're not doing anything this afternoon, are you?" Mary Lou asked.

Samuel's heart sank as both women fixed their gaze upon him. He didn't want to lie, but neither did he want to spend any time with Magnolia. He found her whiny and spoiled. "Actually, I am busy with something else this afternoon."

"Oh." Magnolia hung her head while Mary Lou looked disappointed.

"What is it you're doing?" Mary Lou asked. "Perhaps Magnolia can go along with you."

"*Nee*, it's okay, Mary Lou. I'm sure he's too busy to take me anywhere. I'll just stay home while your parents go visiting and you go off with Jacob."

"Nonsense, you'll have to come with me and Jacob. Jacob won't mind. We're practically married. Our courting days are nearly over. This'll be our last Sunday together before we're a married couple. I'm sure Jacob won't mind sharing that time with you. After all, you are my cousin and soon to be his cousin."

"Are you sure?" Magnolia asked.

He couldn't burden his brother with having Magnolia tag along with them. He knew his brother wanted to spend every moment alone with Mary Lou. He bit the inside of his mouth, still concerned about Catherine. It would be the worst thing in the world for his chances with her if he offered to take Magnolia anywhere. "You could stay on for the singing tonight," he suggested

Magnolia shook her head. "I don't go to those anymore. They're only for the young."

He chuckled. "Around these parts you don't have to be young for the singings. They're for the young and old, mainly for the singles."

"*Jah*, she's single."

He stared at Mary Lou and felt like she was making out that he was asking if she was single. "Well, you'd enjoy the singing, Magnolia." *Can't they take the hint?* He didn't want to be rude.

"Jacob and I aren't staying on," Mary Lou said.

"I'll just go home. It's okay, Mary Lou. Don't worry about me."

Magnolia looked so sad that he felt awful, but he still wasn't prepared to go out with a girl just to be polite and risk losing Catherine's interest. Since Catherine had made the move to sit with him and talk with him, he took that as a sign she might like him. With Mary Lou and Magnolia staring at him, he sat there not knowing what to say and wishing he was as outgoing as his brothers. Any one of them would know what to say, even Benjamin, the youngest.

He looked down at his empty plate and wondered what Benjamin would say. Benjamin would most likely offer to show her around. He probably wouldn't care if he ruined his chances because he didn't see one girl as better than another—he liked them all. Bad example. His mind went next to his most respected brother, Isaac, the oldest. Isaac had held out for the girl he loved even though everyone thought he should marry Mary Lou, the girl he'd been dating for years.

With his older brother's example strong in his mind, he grabbed his plate, stood, and slid off the long bench seat. "I hope you both enjoy the rest of your day." He gave them each a smile and a polite nod before he walked away to put his plate with the other dirty dishes.

CHAPTER 8

"WELL, THAT WAS RUDE!" Magnolia said as she stared at Mary Lou in astonishment.

"It was rather rude. You're right. I was certain he'd offer to show you around. Anyone else would've." She shook her head. "Jacob won't be happy with his behavior."

"You're not going to say anything, are you?"

"*Nee*, I don't want to come in the middle of family. Family is very important to me and to the Fullers. I won't mention anything to Jacob. He'd be so disappointed in his brother."

"He did say he had something to do."

"I wonder what he's got to do today, on a Sunday afternoon. We can't do much on the Day of Rest except to visit people."

"Is he visiting someone then?"

"Maybe."

Magnolia swivelled her head to look over at him. "Are you sure he's not got a girl friend?"

"Jacob would've told me. We tell each other everything. Perhaps you could follow him and see where he goes."

"*Jah*, good idea. Will you come too?"

"*Nee!* I was only joking. You don't mean to say you'd really follow him, do you?"

"*Jah*, I would."

"That's dreadful."

"I just need to know if I'm wasting my time with him. So, I figure if he's really got somewhere to go, he might like me, and if he just goes home and stays there, I'll know he's not interested and he was lying to me just then."

"You'd really go to those lengths?"

"*Jah*, will you come with me?"

"*Nee*. I don't think it's a good idea, Magnolia. It just feels wrong. Anyway, I couldn't even if I wanted to. Jacob and I are spending time together. We really only have Sunday afternoons for each other at the moment, with his job and my job."

"Okay. Do you think your parents would allow me to take the buggy?"

"Not if you're going to follow someone."

Magnolia giggled. "I won't. I was half joking, just like you were when you suggested it. I know they'll be taking the main buggy, but if I could borrow the other buggy I'll just drive around and fill in time."

"I'm sure they won't mind. Ask them."

"I will."

~

JUST AS SAMUEL had put his plate on the dirty-dishes table, he caught Catherine's eye. She smiled and then looked away. Nella was walking away, and Catherine was by herself. This might be a good opportunity to assert himself. He'd told Magnolia he was busy for the rest of the afternoon. What if he was busy with Catherine—if she was interested? He took a deep breath and walked over to her.

"Hi again."

She giggled softly. "Hi."

"Would you like to do something with me this afternoon? You're probably busy, and that's okay."

"I'd like that."

"You would?" He stared at her, scarcely believing his ears.

"What do you have in mind?"

He cleared his throat. His natural instinct was to say anything she wanted to do, but he wanted to be more of a man and take the lead. "I was thinking we could take a drive down by the river, and after that, we could have coffee at one of the cafés down there."

"That sounds good. I'll just let my folks know where I'm going. Will we go from here or will you collect me from the *haus?*"

"I've come with my folks, so I'll go home with them and get my buggy, and then I'll come for you. Tell your folks I'll have you back home before dark."

"Okay."

He stared at Catherine walking away to speak to her parents. If he had known asking her out would be that easy, he would have done it a long time ago. It was hard to believe that she had actually said yes. Did she understand it was a proper date? Surely, she must have.

He wanted to tell one of his brothers he was going out on a real date with Catherine, but if one of them got wind of it, it might get back to Mary Lou and in turn that would get back to Magnolia. It was obvious Mary Lou was trying to match her cousin with him. They were being far too obvious.

WHEN SAMUEL'S parents pulled up at home after the meeting he said, "I'll unhitch the buggy, *Dat*. Then I'm going out."

"Take this one."

"*Nee*, I'll just take mine."

"Suit yourself. Where are you off to today?"

"I'm going out for a few hours. I should be home by dark."

His father nodded and Samuel was grateful his father didn't pry further. Benjamin had driven himself to the meeting since he was staying on for the singing, so Samuel figured his father probably guessed he was taking a girl out for a ride.

"Are you going to eat before you head off?"

"Nee denke, Mamm. I'll get something on the way."

Once he'd unhitched the family's buggy, he hitched his and then headed down the driveway. He looked both ways before he pulled out on the road, and he saw a buggy in the distance. Figuring he had enough time before it got close, he moved his horse forward onto the road. Checking in the rear-view mirror he saw that the buggy wasn't moving.

He thought no more about it until he went around a few turns in the road and noticed the buggy was way behind him, but following slowly.

He took a shortcut to Catherine's house, a little-used road, and was surprised to see the other buggy had followed him. Now, he was becoming suspicious.

When he pulled into Catherine's driveway he noticed that the buggy stopped a fair distance away. It had to be someone who was following him and his best guess was that it was Magnolia.

Catherine came out of the house when he drew close to it.

He didn't want whatever Magnolia was doing to ruin his day, so he pushed it out of his mind completely and focused his attention on Catherine as she climbed into the buggy with him. After they had greeted each other, he turned his buggy around and headed back down the road. He was half tempted to go right and pass Magnolia sitting in her buggy, but that wasn't the way he was heading. He turned left and concentrated on what Catherine was saying to him instead.

"Where are we going?" she finally asked.

"I thought we'd go down by the river like I said this morning, and maybe take a walk before we go to the café."

"Okay."

CHAPTER 9

THROUGHOUT THEIR THEIR WALK, Samuel had seen nothing of Magnolia. When they sat down in the café, at a table with a good view of the parking lot, that same horse and buggy pulled up. Samuel was curious to verify who'd been following them. He was certain he knew. Then he saw her, and it was Magnolia.

"It's a lovely place here, isn't it?"

Catherine smiled. "It certainly is."

He didn't want to mention that they had been followed by Magnolia because it would sound like he had tickets on himself to think that another girl liked him, but what other reason could there be for Magnolia following them? The whole thing was weird. It was weird for Mary Lou to have given him such large hints to show Magnolia around the town. She would already have seen the town anyway when she'd visited before.

As Catherine was chattering away to him, he listened, but out of the corner of his eye, he kept following Magnolia. He wasn't too happy to see her heading right for them.

"Catherine, and Samuel."

Catherine looked around. "Hello, Magnolia. What are you doing out this way?"

"Whenever I come to stay with Mary Lou I get a bit lonely because she's always working. She's with Jacob today and I find myself at a loose end. I've been just driving around and driving around, and then I saw this place and I thought I would have something to eat here."

After a moment of silence, Samuel felt he had no choice but to invite her to sit with them. "You could join us if you'd like to."

"You don't mind?"

"*Nee*, we don't mind at all," said Catherine.

"Okay, *denke*."

Samuel did mind. He minded a great deal, in fact. This was the first proper date he'd ever had, one that he would remember for ever and now he'd have memories of Magnolia crashing his date. She sat next to Samuel, leaned across both of them and grabbed a menu.

"Now let me see. What are you two having?"

"We haven't got that far yet," Samuel said, passing a menu to Catherine and keeping one for himself.

Magnolia giggled. "I thought you would've been here for a while."

Samuel didn't say anything, but he knew that Magnolia knew exactly how long they'd been there.

After they ordered their meals, Samuel wondered exactly what Magnolia hoped to achieve. Did she simply want to ruin things between himself and Catherine, so the way would be made clear for herself? He'd never be interested in a manipulating woman like that. He felt like calling her out and saying he knew that she had been following them, but that would've embarrassed Catherine and made him look like a real jerk. The only thing he could do was keep silent.

"What did you think of what the bishop spoke about this morning?" Magnolia looked at Samuel and then looked at Catherine.

"Very interesting, as always," Catherine said.

"I don't know if it's always possible to forgive others. If they do something really bad, I think you could pretend to forgive them, but is that enough?" Magnolia asked.

"Has someone wronged you in an unforgivable way?" Samuel asked.

"*Nee*, I'm just wondering. That's what I do every time after I hear a sermon. I try and remember what the speaker said and run examples through my head of how I would react in certain situations."

"And does that help?" asked Catherine.

"Help to what?" Magnolia slumped over and rested both elbows on the table.

"Help you … I don't know, be a better person?"

Immediately Magnolia straightened. "Do you think I need to be a better person?"

"*Nee*, no more than anyone else, but I think we all strive against our fleshly nature. That's all I was saying, or rather, meaning."

"Some more than others, maybe." Then Magnolia laughed and looked from one to the other. "Oh, you two; you aren't on a date, are you?" She spoke much louder than was necessary.

It was clear Catherine didn't know what to say as her mouth opened in shock and then she looked at him. If he admitted to being on a date, then word would get around and everybody would know. Being the man, he was supposed to be in charge of the situation, so Catherine would respect him. He had to say something. "We're on a date, but we're also friends, so there's no reason you can't join us."

"That's right, we don't mind at all," Catherine said.

"As long as you're both sure. I'm so sorry." She deliberately made an obvious show of making her body tremble. "It's just that I didn't see the two of you together. I wouldn't have thought you would be a couple." Samuel then looked over at Catherine.

Now, Samuel was getting a little annoyed. Was she forcing one of them to say that it was just a first date?

"This is what you had to do this afternoon and you

wouldn't say what it was," Magnolia said to him, almost accusingly.

Samuel cleared his throat. "I'm just trying to be a gentleman, Magnolia. I didn't want anyone to know where I was going. And it wasn't my place to speak on Catherine's behalf. I didn't want everyone to know our private concerns."

"Jah, quite right. You're quite right."

"You should stop by my home sometime, Magnolia," Catherine suggested. "I get lonesome through the day now that my older sisters are married."

"Denke, that's very kind. Do you really mean that?"

"Of course, I do."

"Would you like it if I visited you tomorrow?"

"That would be lovely. Do you have any sewing with you? We can sew together. That would be fun."

"Jah, I've brought some projects with me."

"Don't you have to help with the wedding?" Samuel asked Magnolia. "It's on Wednesday."

"Mmm, that's true. I'll have duties all day Tuesday, but I might be able to sneak away tomorrow morning."

Sneak was an appropriate word. Samuel figured Magnolia did a lot of sneaking, and she was definitely up to something right now.

"Wunderbaar." Catherine said. "And I'll come over and help with the food on Tuesday. Mary Lou said she didn't need any help, but I must be able to do something."

Then the waiter brought their food and drinks.

"I'll eat this really fast. I feel so bad about not knowing you were on a date."

"Relax, it's fine," Catherine said.

"Don't get indigestion," Samuel said with a laugh as though her being there didn't bother him. He bit into his steak sandwich, and couldn't wait for Magnolia to leave.

Minutes into their meal, Magnolia was getting her spaghetti bolognaise down the front of her clothes. Samuel pretended not to notice because he was annoyed that she needed the attention on her all of the time. That's how he felt. Catherine noticed the mess and handed Magnolia a paper napkin.

"Oh, I'm getting this everywhere. I do this all the time when I eat spag bol. It's my favorite food but it just goes everywhere."

"I'm the same. It helps to put your spoon to the side and then twirl the spaghetti around on the fork with the help of the spoon," Catherine said.

"How?"

Catherine demonstrated how to do it while Samuel grew more annoyed with Magnolia taking over their whole conversation.

"Like this?"

"That's right."

Magnolia pushed some into her mouth and when her mouth was still full she said, "That's a lot better."

Catherine went back to eating her chicken salad.

When Magnolia was finished, she said, "That wasn't

quite enough for me. I wonder if I should be greedy and have seconds."

"Go ahead if you want," Catherine said.

"*Nee,* I should leave you two alone. Are you both having dessert?"

"We're going to a different place for dessert," Samuel said.

"Where are you going?" Magnolia asked.

"We haven't quite decided yet."

"I should go anyway. And leave you alone." She looked at both of them and then giggled. "I never would have thought you two … never mind."

Magnolia went to get money out of the small purse she brought with her, but Samuel said, "It's my treat."

"*Nee,* I couldn't let you do that."

"I insist."

"Really?"

"*Jah.*"

"*Denke* very much and I'll see you tomorrow, Catherine."

"I look forward to it."

And with that, Magnolia stood up and headed back to her buggy.

"I'm sorry about that," Samuel said. "I'll have to make it up to you with another date that's just the two of us."

Catherine said, "That's fine."

"Does that mean there won't be a second date?" he blurted out.

"There will, if you want one."

"*Jah*, please."

Catherine gave a little giggle. Magnolia hadn't ruined everything for them. In fact, by providing some conversation and a buffer, there hadn't been any awkward moments between himself and Catherine.

CATHERINE DIDN'T SAY anything to Samuel, but she knew Magnolia had followed them and in doing so she had deliberately ruined their date.

When they were finally alone, Catherine said, "Do you really want to go somewhere else for dessert? The desserts here look quite good."

"Okay, if that's what you'd like."

He gave her a big smile and then she knew that he had just told Magnolia that they were going somewhere else because he didn't want Magnolia to stay longer.

After they had ordered, Catherine asked him about Timothy.

"He's not doing so good, but he'll come 'round."

"He will be coming back to the community, then?"

"*Jah*, I believe so; he just needs to sort himself out and then he'll be okay."

CHAPTER 10

SAMUEL WALKED into Mary Lou's family home along with his family for Mary Lou and Jacob's wedding. After he and Benjamin sat down, Samuel looked around. It seemed odd that people were single and then, all of a sudden, they started pairing up.

"I hope we see some new talent here today," Benjamin said.

"Aren't there enough women here for you, Benjamin?"

"Not by a long shot. I'm gonna make sure I choose my *fraa* carefully and to do that I need to meet a lot of women. A lot more than are in this community."

"*Mamm* says that *Gott* provides. And that usually the men are able to find *fraas* within their own community. That's just the way *Gott* works."

"Don't you see that *Mamm* made that up, hoping

that we'll be happy with what's here and we won't move away? They want to keep an eye on us forever and that's why *Dat's* worked so hard to grow the business so we'll all have jobs."

Samuel stared at his brother, amazed. He had no idea Benjamin thought that way. "They're just doing their best."

"Yeah, their best at making sure we stick around, but what if my perfect woman is in Canada?"

Samuel chuckled. "Canada?"

"Jah."

Samuel shook his head. He had his little brother figured all wrong; it sounded like he was going to be far choosier then Samuel had thought. "What about Mary Lou's cousin?"

His face lit up. "Mary Lou's got a cousin? Is she here?"

"You've met her. It's Magnolia."

"Ah, her. I thought you meant someone else."

For a moment, Samuel was hoping he might be able to kill two birds with one stone. "I guess she's too old for you anyway."

"I don't mind an older girl, but I don't think I'm suited to Magnolia."

"It's just going to be you and me in the *haus* now until Timothy gets back."

"I know, I've thought of that. It'll be way too quiet. You're not leaving soon, are you?"

"Of course not, who would I possibly marry?"

"Do you want to talk about that date with Catherine?"

Samuel was caught out. He smiled and rubbed his jaw.

"I heard a rumor that you had lunch with two girls the other day." Benjamin chuckled.

"Cut it out. It wasn't like that."

"No? What was it like?"

"I'm not going to tell you. With the mood you're in, anything I say you'll take the wrong way."

Benjamin moved around to face Samuel more squarely. "Try me. I'm a good listener."

Samuel looked around the room. It didn't look like anything was going to start any time soon because people were still coming in and taking their seats. Benjamin wasn't really serious and he always liked to laugh, but there was one thing about him and that was that he could keep a secret. "Okay, but you must keep this to yourself. I took a girl out on Sunday afternoon."

"Don't you mean two?"

"*Nee.*"

"Is that so?"

"Don't look so shocked."

"This is a big deal. This is the first time you've taken a girl out. Was it a real date?"

"*Jah,* it was."

"Who was it?"

"It doesn't matter who it was. If you'll be quiet and stop asking questions I'll tell you what happened. If the wedding starts before I finish I'm not going to revisit it, so be quiet and listen."

"I'm all ears."

"Okay, I'll tell you what happened and how you heard I had lunch with two girls. It was just meant to be the one I like and then—"

"Catherine Miller?" Benjamin whispered.

"*Jah*. I'll start at the beginning. I was at the meeting when I asked her out, and she said yes, and then I had to go home to get my buggy. I go home and pull out of the driveway and start down the road, but then I ..." Samuel told him the whole story.

"So, you were at the café at the stage when you knew it was her for sure?"

"That's right. And we were sitting near a window with a view of the parking lot. She comes in and interrupts us and sits down and has lunch with us. I mean, I had to ask her to join us."

"Magnolia's the one spreading the rumor."

"About me having lunch with two girls?"

"*Jah*."

Samuel put his head in his hands. He didn't like being the subject of gossip. "Why is she doing all this?"

"It's called an obsession. She's obsessed with you, I'd reckon."

"She's got no reason to be obsessed with me. I've only talked to her once or twice."

"I said it's an obsession, I didn't say it was logical. Obsessions have nothing to do with logic. It's what goes on in the person's mind that counts." He tapped a finger on his temple.

"Then she as good as invited herself to Catherine's place the next day. Well, to be fair, she didn't invite herself, but she went on and on about how she gets lonely when Mary Lou is working, so Catherine invited her to her house."

"I can't believe you like Catherine Miller. If you marry her then the three Miller girls would've married three of us."

Samuel put his finger up to tell his brother to be quiet. "It's not for public knowledge. I'd like to have a little bit of privacy before people start putting pressure on us. People would think it was cute ... what you just said."

"I won't say anything about it." Benjamin eyes grew round as he looked at the doorway and Samuel turned around to see what he was staring at. It was Taylor walking into the house with Timothy.

A hush went across the crowd in the house. It was as though everyone knew about Timothy and Taylor. It was an awkward scene and Samuel felt bad for Timothy and Taylor. "I should go and say hello to them."

"Okay, I'll save your seat."

Before Samuel got there, Jacob was talking to them.

Samuel turned around and went back to his seat. "Jacob is talking to them," he told Benjamin.

"They look cute together."

"It's true, they kinda do." He turned around to have another look at them and Magnolia caught his eye and smiled. He gave her a quick polite smile and turned back around to face the front.

CHAPTER 11

AFTER THE WEDDING CEREMONY, Timothy approached Mary Lou and Jacob at the wedding table.

"Welcome to the family, Mary Lou. Taylor mentioned you went over to see her. You just knocked on her door with no warning, or anything."

"*Jah*, I did. I haven't made things worse, have I? Because I was only trying to help. I invited her here today."

A smile spread over his face. "Everything is fine. She said she would come with me to the wedding."

Jacob said, "It seems that things are heading in a better direction for you."

"I hope so."

"Phew. I'm so relieved. I thought you were going to be very cranky with me."

"I'm pleased she's here today. Thanks for inviting

her, Mary Lou. It seems to me all that was needed was the female touch."

Mary Lou was pleased that she had been able to help any member of the Fuller family. She didn't think it likely that Taylor would join the community, but she had felt compelled to try to help.

"It's a step in a good direction, Timothy," Jacob said.

"There's a long way to go yet. She hasn't told her family anything about me. I think they'd hate to know I'm Amish.

~

SAMUEL FOUND BENJAMIN, "Hey, you know what we talked about just now?"

"Let me guess; you mean about you liking Catherine?"

"You got it. I was wondering if you would do me a big favor."

Benjamin stared at him and casually folded his hands across his chest and leaned his weight to one side. "It depends what it is."

"I'd really, really appreciate it."

"Stop trying to sell it and tell me what it is."

Samuel rubbed his forehead. "I told Catherine I owe her a proper date, one that won't be interrupted, and that's where you come in. Can you keep Magnolia occupied while I go on a date with Catherine?"

"I suppose I could do that. How am I supposed to keep her occupied?"

"I don't know."

"I could find out when all the young people are going out to dinner next and invite her along."

"Then I'll arrange the date on that night."

"I suppose I could do that. As long as she doesn't think she's going on a date with me."

Samuel chuckled. "I had thought of that as the favor, but I knew you wouldn't agree."

"You're right about that." Benjamin shook his head. "She's not the girl for me!"

"Off you go and find somewhere to invite her. I want to ask Catherine out today, while we're here at the wedding if possible."

"Talk about pressure."

"Don't waste time standing here talking to me."

"I'm going." Benjamin walked away dragging his feet. "I'll see what I can find out."

Samuel was pleased that he could always rely on his brothers, no matter what the situation.

Until Benjamin came back with a time for the next young people's dinner, he wanted to avoid Catherine. The next time he saw her he wanted to be able to ask her out again. The dinners were held fortnightly and were usually at each other's houses, but sometimes they went out to eat as a group.

Samuel had successfully kept out of everybody's

way and ten minutes later Benjamin returned with a crooked smile on his face.

"What's up?" Samuel asked him.

"I forgot to ask, but exactly what is in this for me?"

"My adoration and appreciation for being a good *bruder*. What more could you want?"

"A handshake and a smile, and a similar favor if ever I need it."

"Done." Samuel offered his hand and Benjamin shook it.

"On Tuesday night, everyone is going to Trisha Yoder's *haus*."

"Perfect," Samuel said, looking around for Catherine.

"That's not all."

Samuel's eyes snapped back to his brother.

"Peter Yoder and I have arranged to collect Magnolia together, and we'll both take her home again."

The dinner was happening at Peter's parents' house, as he was Trisha's brother.

"Perfect." Samuel slapped his brother on the back. "That way she won't be able to go anywhere and she'll be stuck there until you take her home."

"That's exactly right and what's more, she can't take things the wrong way and think I'm taking her on a date or anything because Peter will be with me."

Samuel laughed. "You've got all your bases covered."

"I'm not just a pretty face," Benjamin said with a smirk.

"You can say that again."

"Not just—"

Samuel put his hand up. "Enough."

Benjamin chuckled. "Go and find your girl and ask her out."

"I'll do that right now." Samuel saw Catherine talking to a group of girls and stood nearby and when he caught her eye, he smiled and jerked his head. She took the hint and left the group.

His nerves kicked in as she approached him. He resolutely pushed them away. "Remember how I promised you another date?"

"*Jah.*"

"How does this Tuesday night sound?"

"I could do that. The young people are going to the Yoders' and I told them I would go, but they won't notice if I'm not there."

"Good. How about we keep this just between the two of us?"

Catherine giggled. "Okay."

"Shall I collect you from your *haus* at six?"

"You don't mind if my parents find out?"

"I don't mind if they know. I'm just trying to stop other people from knowing, to keep our date from being disrupted again."

"Okay. Six is fine."

"I'll be looking forward to it."

She gave him a big smile. "Me too."

They went their separate ways.

"WHAT DID HE WANT?"

Catherine swung around to see Magnolia. "He just asked how I'm enjoying the wedding."

"How thoughtful. Are you going to dinner with the young people on Tuesday night?"

"I don't think so. I've had too many late nights."

"What's wrong with that? You don't have a job so you can sleep in."

"No matter what time I go to sleep I still wake up at five o'clock. That's how my body clock is arranged. I know it's silly, but I've always been that way."

"Well, I'm going and guess who's collecting me?"

"Who?"

"Two young men. That's right, two of them." Magnolia giggled. "They're too young for me, but I think both of them like me."

"Who are they?"

"They are Peter Yoder and Benjamin Fuller."

Catherine was a little surprised. "That's nice of them."

"They're collecting me and driving me home again."

"That's good. Are you staying with Mary Lou's parents until she comes back?"

"I don't have any particular plans. I've left it open-ended. My father is not too well and that's why my parents didn't come to the wedding."

"Oh, I'm sorry to hear that. What's wrong with him?"

"It's nothing. He just hurt his leg and can't walk too well. That's why they have to stay at home. *Mamm* would've been able to come by herself, but she never goes anywhere without my *vadder*."

"My parents are the same," Catherine said.

"I should go. I'm helping with the food. I would have thought Mary Lou would make me an attendant seeing that I'm her cousin and everything, but she didn't."

It was dangerous to make a comment on that, so Catherine just nodded.

When their conversation had come to an end, Catherine walked away, and then she looked back at Mary Lou and Jacob. They were certainly well matched. They were both outgoing and confident. Samuel was nothing like any of his brothers. He was much quieter than all six of them.

Over the past couple of years, Catherine had quieted herself down because it seemed everybody had told her she was too outspoken. She was learning to stop and think before she spoke, and she had learned to be more tactful.

Then her attention turned to the *Englischers* at the wedding. There were usually some *Englischers* at every Amish wedding these days, and the ones at this wedding were Taylor and some people the Fullers knew from doing business with them.

Taylor and Timothy looked good together, but Catherine hoped that Timothy wouldn't stay out of the community because of that girl. Perhaps, she would join their community.

~

THIS WAS the happiest day of Mary Lou's life. This was more than her happy ending. She had a husband, a home of her own, and if God willed it, they would have many *kinner* together.

Mary Lou blinked back tears. God had blessed her even though she hadn't had the best personal life in past years. She tried to make up for it now by being nice to people and doing good deeds. All she could do was try her very best.

Taylor looked happy to be at the wedding with Timothy. Mary Lou was pleased with herself for personally inviting her.

CHAPTER 12

AT THE END of the night on Samuel's second date with
Catherine, he had something special to ask her. It
would mean they'd be seen as an official couple, if she
accepted. "Catherine, would you come to Benjamin's
eighteenth birthday with me?"

"I'd love to. When is it?"

"On February fourteen. St Valentines Day."

Catherine giggled. "Is it at your parents' house?"

"Jah. It'll only be the family and they'd know how I
feel about you." He gulped hoping he hadn't over-
stepped the mark.

Catherine couldn't help smiling.

"Don't be bringing a present or anything."

"What about something small?"

"Nee, he'd be embarrassed. We don't give gifts in our
family. Not for birthdays. We give small gifts at
Christmas."

"Okay. I'm looking forward to it."

He stared into her eyes. "Me too." He never imagined that he'd get along so well with a young woman. It was all much easier than he thought it would be.

～

WHEN MAGNOLIA CAME to sew at Catherine's house the next day, they got talking about Benjamin.

"I've overheard Benjamin is having a birthday party." Magnolia giggled loudly.

"It's only going to be a dinner at his parents' *haus*."

"You're going?"

Catherine couldn't tell a lie, but she was tempted. "*Jah*."

"Goody! Will we bring gifts?" From what she said, Catherine wondered if somebody might have invited her, but who?

"I don't know. Maybe. I mean, I don't think he wants gifts."

"Surely we should get him a combined present?"

"*Nee—*"

"I'll get one for him all by myself."

"*Nee*."

"You do what you want and I'll do what I want."

Catherine shook her head. "Okay."

THE NEXT TIME Catherine saw Samuel she wasn't brave enough to tell him that Magnolia expected to go to Benjamin's birthday dinner. After all, what could be done? She couldn't be uninvited because she'd never been invited. She'd have to hope for the best, and that was that Magnolia wouldn't end up going.

～

CATHERINE SAT at the large wooden dining table in the Fullers' kitchen, and there was a knock on the door. She had hoped Magnolia had forgotten all about the birthday because she hadn't mentioned it over the last few days.

From her position at the table, she could see the doorway, and when Mrs. Fuller opened the door Magnolia stood there holding a large cake.

"Magnolia! I didn't expect you here," Mrs. Fuller said.

There was complete silence, and then Magnolia said, "Oh, I'm sorry. I thought it was an open invitation."

Ever the gracious hostess, Mrs. Fuller recovered quickly and said, "It doesn't matter. There's always room for one more at our *haus*."

"Now I'm embarrassed."

"Don't be. You know everyone here and your friend, Catherine, is here too."

"I brought cake– birthday cake."

Mrs. Fuller took the cake from her outstretched hands. "This looks lovely. I'll place it in the center of the table. Come with me."

Magnolia followed Mrs. Fuller into the house. "Now, you know Hazel and Isaac, Adeline and Joshua, Lucy and Levi?"

"I do." She smiled at everyone.

"And my little *boppli bu,* Abe."

"He's not so little anymore," Hazel said, trying to hold him in her arms as he struggled to get down.

"Look at this lovely cake," Mrs. Fuller said, placing the cake in the center of the table. It was two layers; the top layer was smaller than the first and it almost looked like a wedding cake. The frosting was pale pink with pale blue stripes.

While everyone commented on the fine cake, Isaac hurried away and came back with an extra chair that he placed beside Benjamin.

Benjamin smiled at her as she sat beside him. *"Denke* for coming, Magnolia."

"I just explained to your *mudder* that I didn't know it was a family dinner. I'm so embarrassed."

"Nee, don't be," Lucy said. "The more people, the better."

"Especially if all those people bring cake," Benjamin joked.

"You're always welcome here," Mr. Fuller said. "Whatever the day."

"And you have your birthday on St Valentines Day, Benjamin," Magnolia said.

"Very fitting." He smiled. "And *denke* for the cake. *Mamm's* are always yummy, but I've never had one so grand-looking as this."

Magnolia said, "I made it myself. I love baking cakes and frosting them. I was going to have you help me, Catherine, but I haven't seen much of you these last few days."

"*Nee,* that's true. I'm not sure why."

Mrs. Fuller then joined them at the table. "We should say grace if everyone will please stop their chatter."

Everyone did, and they all closed their eyes and said their silent prayers of thanks for the food.

When everyone had finished, Mr. Fuller said, "And a special thank you to *Gott* for Benjamin. He's brought laughter and joy to all of us over the years."

Benjamin chuckled. "*Denke, Dat.* It's nice to hear something positive said about me."

As everyone started passing the food around, Benjamin's brothers were making good-humored jokes about him. Catherine wasn't really listening because she was too worried about what Magnolia was up to. This was her first meal at the Fullers' as Samuel's girl-friend and she was doing her best not to be annoyed that Magnolia was there. Perhaps she should've told her that the dinner was a small one, just family, but then Magnolia would've known that things were more serious between her and Samuel and she wasn't ready for Magnolia, or anyone, to know.

Things at the table got much quieter around dessert time. Baby Abe was asleep on a couch in the living room and they were discussing when to eat Magnolia's cake.

"I have another cake in the kitchen, but this one's so nice that I've decided to make yours his official birthday cake," Mrs. Fuller told Magnolia.

"I didn't mean to do that. Now I feel awful."

"Nonsense, cake never goes astray in this household."

Magnolia giggled, puffing out her full cheeks.

Mr. Fuller reached out and picked up the cake knife from the center of the table. He smiled and handed it to Benjamin. "You might as well cut it now."

"It looks too lovely to cut," Hazel said, smiling at the cake.

"Lovely, yes," said Benjamin with a laugh, "but cake is never too lovely to cut and to eat."

CATHERINE FOUND herself starting to relax when dinner was almost over. Relief came when it was time for the ladies to clear the table. Mrs. Fuller's daughters-in-law suggested their mother-in-law go into the living room with the men and be with Benjamin for his birthday, and the young women would wash the dishes. Catherine and Magnolia joined in the work.

As they scraped food scraps off the plates and prepared for the washing up, Magnolia said to Lucy, "You and Adeline have been married for a while now. I'd reckon Mrs. Fuller would be waiting on more *grosskinner.*"

Catherine stared wide-eyed at Lucy, hoping she wouldn't be upset by Magnolia's tactless remark. Instead of seeing shock on her sister's face, Catherine saw a secret smile.

"Well, if you can all keep a secret ..."

Adeline rushed to her side. "Are you?"

Lucy nodded. "It's only early and we didn't want to say anything just yet, not for a few more weeks."

"I'm so happy for both of you," Magnolia said.

Catherine stepped forward, annoyed that Magnolia had butted in and found out this exciting news at the same time as she did. After all, she was Lucy's sister, not Magnolia. "Me too." Each girl hugged Lucy in turn.

WHEN HAZEL WALKED into the kitchen after checking on Abe they told her the news and she had news of her own to add. Hazel was expecting her second baby. There was so much giggling and excitement that Hazel had to shush them all. "We don't want anyone to know just yet either."

Magnolia stared at Adeline. "You'll be left behind."

Catherine was shocked yet again. What an insensitive comment!

Adeline pulled a face. "We're hoping for a *boppli* soon, too. It's in *Gott's* hands."

"That's right," Hazel said. "It'll happen."

CHAPTER 13

A COUPLE OF DAYS LATER, Mr. Fuller drove his younger boys into work. Isaac was now running Fuller & Sons Joinery, but that didn't stop their father from being there every day to make sure things ran smoothly. Benjamin was unusually quiet this morning, and Samuel knew that there was something wrong with him.

When their father was tending their horse in the parking lot, Samuel gave Benjamin a little shove. "Hey, what's wrong with you?"

"If you must know, your friend, Magnolia, is spreading rumors."

"About me?"

Benjamin sighed. "No, about me."

"What are the rumors?"

"Apparently, I'm dating her. Can you imagine it?

She is way too old for me, and she is definitely not my type."

"How do you know the rumors are coming from her?"

"Just a wild stab in the dark. And I don't think I'm wrong, not after your tale of her tailing you and Catherine on your first date."

"Why would she be doing that to you?"

"Isn't it obvious?"

Samuel stared at his brother. "Not to me it isn't."

"She's obviously in love with me. Or she thinks she is. I know you think she was in love with you because she was following you and all, but maybe she was trying to get close to you to get to me."

Samuel shook his head. "It's all a bit confusing for me."

"Either way, following you was a very weird thing to do."

Samuel pushed the door of the factory open. "It was. Let's not mention this to anyone else."

"I won't. Believe me, the fewer people who know about this, the better. How will I get a girl my own age if everyone thinks I'm dating Magnolia?"

"I know." Samuel could see that, to Benjamin, this was the worst thing in the world. And he couldn't disagree. Magnolia was an unusual girl, and not unusual in a good way.

"And why did she come to my birthday dinner?" he whispered.

"I have no idea. It was a shock to me when she turned up."

"It just makes the rumors more believable."

"Put it out of your mind while you're at work, and tomorrow I'll see what I can find out. Magnolia is fairly close with Catherine, so I'll find out if she knows anything."

"Denke."

"Cheer up."

Benjamin pulled a face. "I'll try."

SAMUEL STOPPED by Catherine's house after work and they sat in the living room together.

"Is something wrong?" Catherine asked.

He nodded. "Benjamin is upset because there are rumors going around about him and Magnolia."

"You mean rumors that they are together, or something?"

"Jah. And he thinks that the rumors are coming from Magnolia herself."

Catherine frowned. "Really?"

"Well, that's what he thinks."

"I wonder why she'd do that."

"Why would she come to his birthday party without being invited?"

"That might've been my fault."

His eyebrows drew together. "Why's that?"

"She said she had heard there was a birthday party, and I said it wasn't a party as such, it was just a birthday dinner." Catherine shrugged. "Then she asked if I was going and I said yes because I couldn't lie about it. Remember, no one knows about the two of us dating, so she wouldn't have thought I would've gotten a special invitation. I guess that she assumed that since I was going it was just an open invitation to come to the birthday."

"I see how she could have possibly been mixed up."

"I'm sure she felt bad when she got there and realized it was a family dinner. Your *mudder* made her feel welcome, though."

"*Jah, Mamm* is like that. Have you told your sisters about us?"

"I didn't have to do, they guessed."

Samuel chuckled. "They were bound to find out sooner or later. Can I see you this Saturday?"

"*Jah,* I'd like that."

"We can spend the whole day together."

"Can we have a picnic? I can pack us a basket."

He couldn't help smiling at how excited she was. "That sounds *wunderbaar.*"

ON SATURDAY, Samuel collected Catherine so they could spend the day together. She already knew he was her perfect match. In spite of him being one of the

Fullers, and her older sisters being married to two of his older brothers, his shyness was the only reason he hadn't occurred to her as a potential suitor.

She glanced over at him and he looked back at her and gave her a big smile. He didn't just smile with his perfectly-shaped mouth; even his dark eyes were smiling in a warm and genuine manner.

He looked out the window at the golden glow of the sun as it warmed the late-winter-chilled fields. "I'm looking forward to the warmer weather."

"Me too. Even though it wasn't all that cold this winter."

"Not as cold as some."

"I was hoping Timothy might have come to Benjamin's birthday."

"He hasn't been around much lately. It was a wonderful surprise to have him come to the wedding."

"You must miss him."

"I do, a lot, but he's been gone a long time now and it's just me and Benjamin at home with our parents. We've grown a bit closer now that it's just the two of us."

"Now you know how I feel with both of my sisters married. It's just me in the house now, and I really miss their company. Just me and *Mamm* do all the chores. Not that there's much to do now with just three of us. There's a lot less washing in the house and the meals are half the size."

Samuel chuckled. "Our meals are a small fraction of

the size they used to be. *Mamm* still makes a lot in case we have visitors, and we very often do."

"We don't have many visitors. Have you ever thought about going on *rumspringa?*"

"I've thought about it, but I decided not to. What about yourself?" He glanced over at her.

"I'm happy where I am. Things didn't go so good for Mary Lou when she left the community for a time."

"Well, that was a little different because she'd been baptized so when she left she wasn't on *rumspringa.*"

"I know, but she had such a hard time of it when she came back. She told my sisters about it. She was often over at our house, before and after she'd been shunned." Catherine thought she'd better add, "Not while she was shunned. Anyway, I'm glad she married Jacob. They're such a good match."

"It was a little bit of a shock to me. I just didn't see the two of them together. I think Jacob liked a lot of girls before he settled on Mary Lou."

"You mean a lot of girls liked him."

Samuel laughed. "That's what Jacob kept telling me."

"All your brothers have been popular with girls."

He shrugged. "I don't know about that."

"That's how it seems to me."

"They were married older than most. It took them some time to settle on who they wanted to marry."

"Sometimes it pays to be choosy," she said.

"You have to be choosy. Are you trying to tell me something?"

"*Nee*, like what?" She giggled.

"Are you choosy?"

"I've only ever gone out with you."

"The same with me and you."

They exchanged smiles.

Contentment once again filled Catherine's heart and she looked over the fields. They weren't bright green, they were a weak yellow-green, but at least all the snow was now gone and the longed-for warm weather was on its way.

"I hope you like where I'm taking you. It's a large park with a beautiful river where we can sit and watch the ducks and even feed them. I've got some bread."

"Is the bread for us or the ducks?"

He chuckled. "You can have some if you like stale bread. It was bread *Mamm* was about to toss, so I grabbed it for the ducks."

"I think I'll give the bread a miss, *denke*."

"Me too. I'm sure you've got something much tastier for us in that basket you've got in the back. It was certainly heavy enough."

"I've got plenty and it's all better than stale bread."

"I hope so. We'll soon find out." Samuel chuckled. "Do you like that kind of thing—just sitting and being still, feeling the sun on your face and a slight breeze on your skin?"

Catherine was tempted to laugh, but she didn't want to offend him. He was certainly a sensitive man.

"Very much so. I'd like to be where no one can find us. Or follow us."

"Especially follow us." He looked over his shoulder and then Catherine also looked behind them. "You knew we were being followed the other day?" he asked her.

"I did, but I didn't know you knew until just now."

"I didn't know for certain until she sat down with us."

"I didn't know what was going on, and I didn't want to be rude to her."

He laughed. "Neither did I."

"I think she liked you and now she's turned her attention to Benjamin. I don't think I'm betraying her confidence because I don't think she's making a secret of it."

"Even if you were betraying her confidence, I won't be telling anyone. Whatever you tell me will be between the two of us."

"Okay, I'll keep that in mind. And you have a secret to tell me?" she asked.

His eyes open wide as he looked over at her. "I might have."

"What is it?"

"Maybe later, when we're sitting by the water."

"Okay. Don't forget now."

"I'm sure you'll remind me."

"I will."

When they got to the river, Samuel pulled the

picnic basket out of the back of the buggy. "It sure is heavy."

"It's just our lunch and something to drink."

"Soda, I hope."

"*Jah*, don't worry. You won't get pulled over on the way home."

"Good." He grinned, and nodded his head to a blanket on the back seat. "Can you grab that blanket?" She leaned in and took hold of it. "You choose the spot," he said.

Catherine spread the blanket on the grassiest spot that she could find in the park, and Samuel put the basket on top. She sat down cross-legged and spread her dress over her knees. Looking up and down the banks of the river, she asked, "Where are all these ducks?"

He sat down with her, looked up and down the water's edge and scratched his head. "They must be hibernating."

She giggled. "Ducks don't hibernate."

"How do you know?"

"They just don't, silly."

He laughed along with her. "Maybe it's too early in the morning for them. I'm sure they'll be along later when you least expect them. Oh, I left the bread in the buggy."

"Don't worry about it. We can go back and get it if they ever show."

"They will. Just you wait and see." He looked up at

the sky that was starting to cloud over. "I hope it doesn't rain."

"It certainly is colder than I thought it would be."

"I've got a coat in the buggy if you'd like it?"

"Nee, I'm all right at the moment, *denke."* She stared at him and smiled.

"What is it?" he asked.

"You're not quiet at all."

"I never said I was."

"I always thought … I mean, I always thought you were very quiet."

"I just don't speak unless I've got something to say. How about we go for a walk so we can work up an appetite for your delicious food?"

She looked around. "Is it okay to leave the food here?"

"There's no one else around for miles. No one is going to steal our food unless the ducks figure out how to open the basket."

He reached out his hand and she put her hand in his.

After he pulled her to her feet, she pulled her hand away and said, "You lead the way."

He walked along to the right and she hurried to walk beside him.

AFTER A WHILE OF WALKING, Catherine said, "There aren't any birds to speak of, only a few chickadees and jays and crows. I think it's far too cold still for most of them to come out."

He suddenly stopped and she did too. "If you're cold, wear this." He started taking off his coat.

She giggled. "I can't because then you'll be cold."

"You take it. I don't feel the cold so much."

Catherine liked the way he was so protective and caring. "Okay."

He held the coat for her while she slid her arms into the sleeves, and then he fixed the collar for her.

She spun around in a circle. "How does it look?"

His face beamed. "Better on you." He started walking again and she walked beside him. "I wonder if the water is cold."

She gave him a playful shove. "Do you want to find out?"

He laughed and held onto her arm. "If you push me in, I'll drag you in along with me."

She pulled her arm away, gave him another shove and ran off ahead of him. She ran along the water's edge, slipped a little and then regained her balance. When she turned around she saw he was closing in on her. She turned away and ran. Suddenly she almost ran into a fence that continued downhill and into the water, and she could go no further. She spun around so fast that she overbalanced, flailed her hands in the air trying to rebalance, and fell into the water. Now, another date was ruined just like their first.

CHAPTER 14

"ARE YOU ALRIGHT?" Catherine heard Samuel call out.

"I'm okay, it's not deep." She stood up and then her foot got caught on something under the water and when she tried to pull it away she fell into the water face first. Then she managed to stand up again. Samuel stepped right into the water, getting wet himself just to rescue her.

Once she was upright facing him, and he had his hands gently resting on her elbows, he said, "If you wanted to go for a swim you should've just said so."

All she could do was laugh. "I'm so sorry, and now you're wet too."

He looked down at her wet clothes. "Only from my knees down. Not like you. We'll have to go take you home to get you out of those wet clothes."

"*Nee*, our day has only just begun. I'm not ready to

go home. We are supposed to be spending the whole day together."

He linked his arm through hers and started moving out of the water. "You really can't stay in those wet clothes. The only solution I can think of, if you would be willing, is that I have a change of clothes in the back of the buggy. You could wear those and there's the blanket in the buggy. Meanwhile, we could spread your dress out in the sun to dry."

She thought about this proposition. There was no sun to speak of, not with those gray clouds looming. No one was around to see her in men's clothing. "Where am I supposed to get dressed?"

"I'll stay here and you can get dressed in the buggy. I won't look."

She put a hand to her head and realized her prayer *kapp* was soaking as well.

"You'll have to take that off as well," he said. "You can cover your head with the blanket."

"Okay." She looked up at the sky. "I only hope it doesn't rain." There was a little bit of sun poking between the clouds. "Where are your dry clothes?"

"Behind the seat. You can't miss them."

"Okay, but stay here and don't look."

"I will. I mean, I will stay here and I won't look." He gave her a smile and then she turned and headed to the buggy.

After she had changed into his dry clothes, she found another blanket in the buggy and wrapped herself in it. When she got out of the buggy, she spread her clothes out across the buggy, and then headed back to Samuel, making sure her head was covered by the blanket.

"Do they fit?"

She shook her head with a laugh. "What do you think? I'm glad you had a belt there. I've never worn clothes like these before."

"At least you're warm and dry now. Shall I see what we have in this surprise basket?"

Catherine giggled about the situation. If they got married it would certainly be a strange story to tell their children and their grandchildren. "It's just fried chicken and a few other things. Nothing too special."

"There's nothing I like better than cold fried chicken."

"I didn't know that."

"It's true," he said as he took the lid off the basket and brought things out.

"There are plates down the side," Catherine said as she sat down. "Oh, I don't know how you wear these."

"I don't know. I've never worn anything else. I don't know how you women can do all of your tasks while wearing dresses. How many pieces of chicken would you like?"

"Just one."

He arranged a plate for her with chicken, sauerkraut and tiny potatoes that were sprinkled with parsley.

She took the plate from him and thanked him. "I hope you also like cold potatoes."

"I do."

"I've got knives and forks somewhere on the bottom there, and also paper napkins."

He handed her a plastic knife and fork and a couple of paper napkins.

"*Denke.* I'll get the soda." Catherine poured the soda and, once they had full plates and drinks in front of them, they started eating. "It's a little uncomfortable using a knife and fork and not being able to eat at a table. It'd be easier to eat with my fingers."

"You can eat with your fingers if you want," he said.

"I don't think so. That would get rather messy."

He chuckled. "Coming from the girl who just fell into the water."

"Yeah, true. I'll never ever live that down, will I?" Catherine giggled.

"Probably not."

As she placed the cold chicken into her mouth, she was grateful for the warm clothes and the blanket around her; the day was becoming colder and not warmer. The sun was still hiding somewhere behind the gray clouds.

"Hopefully that breeze will dry your clothes."

With a mouthful of food, Catherine could only nod, but it had been her experience with drying clothes that a chilling breeze wouldn't go very far in helping clothes dry.

"I should've made hot chocolate, and I would've if I'd known the weather was gonna be this cold."

"Maybe we should take you home and you can change your clothes and then we can go out somewhere closer to home?"

"Okay." She agreed because she wasn't comfortable at all.

He glanced over at the buggy. "I don't think your clothes are going to dry."

"*Nee.*" She gulped nervously. Then she realized that if she went home now, her parents wouldn't be at home because they had plans to be out visiting that day. "We can go home as soon as you're ready."

"I'm ready now. Well, as soon as I eat this. Unless you'd like to go for another swim?"

"Maybe I will." She giggled. "And maybe this time you can come too."

He laughed. "There's only one oversized blanket and you're wearing my spare clothes."

"Otherwise you would, right?"

"Of course. I always love to jump in freezing-cold rivers this time of year."

When they finished their food, Catherine repacked the picnic basket and Samuel helped by putting all the lids back on the containers.

Samuel put the basket in the back and then noticed her prayer *kapp* had been blown a distance away. He picked it up and brought it back. "I'll tie this onto the buggy and the wind will help it dry."

Catherine wasn't too worried about it drying because she would have to wash all her clothes when she got home anyway. She climbed into the buggy next to Samuel.

"We're not going to let your accidental swim ruin our day."

"Okay." When they were halfway home, she noticed her prayer *kapp* was no longer near the rearview mirror where he'd tied it. *"Ach nee."*

"What?"

"My *kapp.*"

He looked over. "It's gone. I'm so sorry. I can't have tied it on well enough."

"It must've worked its way loose." If her parents were home they'd be furious. Although, she had kept her head covered by the blanket. It was bad enough to be in men's clothing, but under the circumstances it was a necessity to keep warm. She closed her eyes and prayed, and hoped that no one would be home.

"Shall we go back and look for it?" Samuel asked.

"Nee. I've got plenty more at home. I think my parents will be out. If you stay in the buggy, I'll just get changed and come back out."

"Okay."

As they approached the house, she saw that her parents were just getting in the buggy to leave.

"This would have to be the worst timing ever," she said, wishing she could disappear into thin air.

"Don't worry. I'll just explain what happened. It'll be okay."

The smile on Samuel's face told Catherine that he knew nothing of her parents. Maybe he was right and they would listen to a reasonable explanation—she hoped. "I guess they wouldn't want me hanging around in wet clothes on a cold day like this."

"Exactly. And that water was freezing."

Her parents stood side-by-side waiting as Samuel's buggy drew closer.

"Stay here and I'll explain what happened."

He jumped out of the buggy and strode toward her parents. Then she saw the look of horror spread across her mother's face when she saw the blanket over her daughter's head. Then her mother's eyes were on Samuel.

After Samuel said a few words, her father marched over to her. When Samuel followed him, she heard him say, "There was a minor accident, but don't worry, Catherine was unharmed."

Mr. Miller ignored him and looked Catherine up and down. "What happened?"

Before she had a chance to speak her mother was also standing in front of her. "Where is your prayer *kapp?*"

"It blew away."

"It blew off your head?"

"Not exactly."

"Get out of the buggy," her mother ordered.

Catherine stepped down from the buggy, still holding the blanket wrapped around her. "Why is that blanket on you?" Her mother pulled her toward the house away from the men.

"I fell in the lake and got wet and freezing cold."

Her mother pulled the blanket aside and saw the white shirt and the black trousers. Her mouth fell open in horror and she didn't speak. Catherine took a step back and then closed the blanket back around herself.

"Go inside. Go directly inside right now!"

Catherine hurried to the house hoping that Samuel would have more of a chance to explain. She ran through the front door and when her mother didn't follow, she looked out the window of the living room. Samuel was being reprimanded by both of her parents at once and her father was talking while his hands were waving about in the air. He only did that when he was really angry. Her mother had her hands firmly on her hips.

Then she saw her father point down the road and when Samuel got back into the buggy, she knew her father was telling him to go. This was dreadful. If only they had waited a little longer before they'd come home then she would have missed her parents altogether and the date would've turned out different. She would've simply changed into dry clothes and resumed their date. Her parents were making far too big a deal out of everything.

When she saw her mother heading to the house, she

ran to her bedroom as fast as she could. As soon as she was in her room, she stepped out of the men's clothes and when she was halfway through pulling on a dress, her door opened.

"What is the meaning of this?"

"I'm putting on my clothes."

Her mother sat on the bed and picked up the discarded shirt and trousers. "You were wearing men's clothing. You changed out of your dress?"

"*Jah,* I'm trying to tell you that I had to because—"

"And where was that boy when you were doing that?"

"I had to get changed out of the wet clothes because it was so cold. I fell in the water and it was freezing."

"Nonsense. You should have wrapped yourself in a blanket and come straight home."

She looked away from her mother knowing that was an option they had considered. Couldn't her mother understand that they wanted to spend time together? "We haven't done anything wrong."

"You had your head uncovered and you were wearing men's clothing and goodness knows what else there is to the story."

"You have to trust me, *Mamm.* Neither of us did anything wrong or even close to it."

"Your *vadder* and I are going out and we will discuss a suitable punishment and we'll talk to you when we get home."

Catherine opened her mouth to say something but

her mother was already out the door and then she heard her walking down the wooden steps.

It was all a big mess. She felt sorry for Samuel. Who knew what they had accused him of?

She finished dressing and then took Samuel's clothes down to the laundry room. The brief time she'd spent with Samuel was the best she'd ever had in her life. He was so thoughtful and she felt so connected to him. Samuel was someone she could have very easily overlooked if Mary Lou and Magnolia hadn't been sent by *Gott* to her house that day. They had kept asking her about him. She placed the clothes in the hamper and then headed into the kitchen. She leaned over the sink and looked out the window. Her parents were already gone, and sadly, so was Samuel.

CHAPTER 15

THE WAY CATHERINE'S mother had talked to her left a bad feeling in the pit of her stomach. Then she realized she had left the picnic basket and her wet clothes in the buggy. Hopefully, Samuel's parents wouldn't have a similar reaction to him arriving home. At least he wouldn't be arriving home wearing women's clothing. Catherine had a little giggle at that thought.

Her mother had never talked to her like that before, and *Mamm's* mind had clearly gone to the worst place. The first part of this day was the best day of her life and the latter part of the day was the worst.

SAMUEL DROVE AWAY FROM THE MILLERS' house fighting back tears. He could see himself married to Catherine.

She'd been the only girl he could really talk seriously with, and they were also able to laugh, have fun and joke around. Now, because he didn't bring her home right after she'd fallen in the water, he'd ruined everything.

It jumped into his mind that in the bible it said not only to abstain from evil but abstain from the appearance of evil. He'd learned a good lesson. He decided to wait for a few days until the Millers calmed down and then he would talk to them and tell them exactly what had happened.

He had seen the rage in Mr. Miller's eyes and the disappointment in Mrs. Miller's. Never having had a girlfriend, he'd never had to contend with a girl's parents before. He should've been more aware of their feelings and their protectiveness over their daughter.

As he traveled homeward in his buggy, something white on the side of the road caught his eye. He pulled his buggy off onto the shoulder, stopped, and jumped out. When he got closer, he saw it was Catherine's prayer *kapp*. He leaned down and picked it up. It was still wringing wet and now it was covered in dirt.

With the soiled *kapp* in his hands he somehow felt closer to Catherine. He turned and walked back to the buggy, dragging his feet all the way. When he got back, he looked over into the back to place the *kapp* in a safe place and then he saw the picnic basket and Catherine's wet clothes. He sighed. He'd have to have his mother wash the clothes before he took them back to her.

Samuel leaned back and laughed. What else could he do? The situation was so tragic and looked so bad, but finally he could see the funny side.

He wondered how he would approach his mother with Catherine's outfit complete with dress, apron, cape and *kapp*. The natural question she would ask was how he came to have them in the first place. He couldn't turn around and take them back to Catherine, not with the way Mr. Miller had told him to get off their property.

All he could do was tell his mother the truth, or learn to work the gas-powered washing machine himself.

"We're going home, Midnight." He clicked his horse forward while still working out what his next move should be. If he washed the clothes in secret, it would look even worse if someone discovered what he was doing.

When he got home, he found his mother in the kitchen, and right at the kitchen table he told her the whole story. All she did was shake her head at him and he felt a fool. "I know, I know, I did the wrong thing. I should've taken her home straightaway."

She nodded and kept staring at him as though she couldn't believe what he'd told her.

"Are you gonna go all mad at me? Yell at me?"

Her eyebrows rose as she drew in a breath. *"Nee.* I think you've learned a good lesson from this."

"I certainly have."

"What have you learned exactly?"

"The first thing we probably shouldn't have done is to go somewhere so deserted."

"Nee you shouldn't have, not if it was only going to be the two of you."

"And we have to be careful how things look to other people," he added hoping to win his mother's approval by his confession and lesson-learning ability.

"We? You mean you and Catherine? So, you plan on seeing her again?"

His jaw dropped open. From how his mother spoke, he thought she thought it a bad idea. *"Jah* I do. When her parents calm down. I had the best time with her."

"That's good. I haven't seen you look this happy since you were five and your brothers were taking you fishing for the first time."

He was relieved. It would be the worst thing if his parents were against him being involved with Catherine. "I didn't know it showed."

"It does. Do you want me to talk to the Millers?"

He shook his head. "I'm old enough that I can handle my own ... situations."

"Very well." She looked at the wet clothes Samuel had placed in the center of the table. "I'll see what I can do about these clothes."

"Denke, Mamm."

It was great that his mother believed him. But his mother would know that he would never lie to her.

"I'll put these in the machine, and then how would you like a cup of hot chocolate?"

"I'd love one."

"Have you eaten?"

"Catherine made the most amazing food." He rubbed his forehead. "That reminds me. Catherine's basket is still in the back of the buggy with all the leftovers and scraps."

"Go fetch it and we'll clean it out. We can't have old food scraps hanging around attracting vermin."

While his mother tended to the clothes he brought the basket into the kitchen and started pulling out the leftovers.

When his mother came back, she said, "You sit down, I'll do that."

"I'll do it. It won't take long."

"*Nee*, I'll do it. You can put the milk on for the hot chocolate."

Samuel was useless in the kitchen because his mother did everything. He didn't know how she made hot chocolate. This was the first time he knew of that she'd allowed one of her sons to do anything in the kitchen, except for a couple of times when she'd been ill. "Are you having one too?"

"*Jah*, put two cups of milk in to boil. Not to boil, to heat," she corrected herself.

"I'll put it on a medium heat."

"Good idea."

He did that and then sat back down, pleased to have

his mother's understanding over what had happened. "I don't know when I should talk to her parents. Do you think I should give them a couple of days to cool down?"

"That might be a good idea and by then Catherine would've had more of a chance to explain to them what happened."

"They certainly didn't give me a chance."

"Your *vadder* would've been the same if he'd had a *dochder*. We were never blessed with any."

"Instead you had seven *wunderbaar* sons."

She looked at him and smiled. "I have been very blessed and I'm not saying I haven't. I feel I would've been closer to a girl and got to experience different things with a girl, but *Gott* didn't bless me with that, but He blessed me in other ways."

He wanted to point out that now she had some daughters-in-law she adored, but he knew she'd say it wasn't the same. *"Denke* for being so understanding, *Mamm."*

She stared at him. "I don't think I am. I'm just more understanding than the Millers."

"Oh?"

She poured the hot milk into the powdered chocolate. "When you get a bit older, you'll see that it was an absolutely stupid thing that you did, and I don't blame Mr. Miller for telling you to go."

"Jah, but you know it's not what it looks like, right?"

"I believe you because that's what you tell me, but

you both put yourself in compromising positions and that's not good."

He thought back again to what had happened. And if he was a different kind of man he could've tried to take advantage of the situation. Now, all he wanted to do was move past it. What had been such a lovely time with the woman his heart desired was now becoming a moment he deeply regretted. He heaved a huge sigh right as his mother placed the hot chocolate in front of him.

"*Denke, Mamm.*"

She sat down opposite. "Drink that and think about what you'll say to the Millers."

All he wanted to do was put it out of his mind.

"I don't know where your *vadder* and I went wrong. There's Timothy and now you."

He took a sip of his hot drink. "Sorry, *Mamm.*" What he'd done was nothing like what Timothy had done, but he could see his mother was starting to think of how the situation would appear to others. He tried to point out the good side of things. "It's good that Timothy went to the wedding along with Taylor."

"She didn't even speak to me, and he didn't speak to me either."

"It would be awkward for both of them. Last time you talked to Timothy things didn't go so well. He probably thought it best to keep his distance at the wedding. At least the both of them were there. That was a good thing, right?"

"I don't know."

He placed his fingertips gently on his mother's arm. "Don't worry. I'll talk to Mr. Miller and I'll sort it all out."

His mother gave him a half-smile and nodded.

CHAPTER 16

CATHERINE WOKE up the next morning and realized that she had fallen asleep early the previous evening and had slept the whole way through without ever talking to her parents. Now it was Sunday morning, and the meetings were always held early. Quickly, she dressed and went down to breakfast. Her mother was sitting by herself at the kitchen table.

"Where's *Dat?*"

"Hitching the buggy. I didn't want to wake you last night. Your *vadder* and I will have a talk with you when we get home from the meeting."

"Good. Then I can tell you both what happened."

"That won't stop you from being grounded."

"Grounded? For real?" Catherine had never been grounded in her life.

"*Jah,* for real."

"How long will I be grounded for?"

"I'm so unhappy about what happened. None of you girls have given me any trouble until you go and do this. Don't you see what you've done is bad? You show up here in men's clothing and with no *kapp*. You would've had to have been undressed while in a young man's company, and you think that's okay? Nothing you can say to me will make me think there's nothing wrong in what you did. And that is if you're telling me the truth about nothing more happening."

"Nothing happened. It's the truth. All I did was change out of wet clothes and into dry ones, by myself inside the buggy, and I kept my head covered with the blanket." When she saw her mother's eyes glaze over, she said, "You must see the Fullers are good people. You allowed Lucy and Adeline to marry Levi and Joshua."

"That's right. And we might not allow our third daughter to marry a third Fuller!"

Catherine's blood ran cold. "You can't be serious."

"Your *vadder* and I agree you're not to go out of the house for three months."

"Three months? You mean three weeks?"

Her mother's jaw clenched and she shook her head. "*Nee*, months."

"You can't be serious."

"We are."

"That's unheard of." Catherine sprang to her feet and wanted to run to her room.

"We don't care. We need to break whatever is

between you and Samuel, and time should do it."

"You think time will do that?"

"*Jah*, he'll tire of waiting."

Catherine collapsed into a kitchen chair, not believing her ears. "Does that mean I won't be allowed to go anywhere?"

"That's right, nowhere. Not even the Sunday meetings."

Now she wouldn't see Samuel today like she thought she would. Catherine sat there staring at her mother wondering if there was anything she could say or do that would make them change their minds. Then she started worrying about what her father would say to Samuel. "What is *Dat* going to say to him today?"

"Just what I said, that he needs to stay away from you."

She shook her head. "I can't believe you're not even allowing me to go to the meeting. If you think I'm some kind of sinner, wouldn't the meeting help me?"

"That's the decision your *vadder* and I have made. You won't be seeing that boy any time soon and if that means you have to stay away from the meetings then you shall stay away from the meetings." Her mother got up and walked out of the kitchen.

SAMUEL SAT IN THE YODERS' living room where the Sunday meeting was being held, while Benjamin sat beside him talking to him. He wasn't hearing a word of what Benjamin was saying; his heart was pumping fast as he was waiting for Catherine to walk in the door. He couldn't wait to see her again.

He hoped her parents hadn't been too hard on her. He looked away when he saw Mrs. Miller walk in and, out of the corner of his eye, he watched for Catherine. When no one else came in behind Mrs. Miller he turned to see if he had missed her. No, there was no Catherine. A few minutes later, Mr. Miller walked in the door and there was still no Catherine. Perhaps she had caught a cold. He would never forgive himself if she had gotten sick while she was with him. He should've taken better care of her. They never should've been fooling around near the water's edge.

When everyone had sat down, the meeting started. Samuel considered leaving, but it would look ten times worse for both of them if he went to Catherine's house knowing that she was there alone. He had no choice but to stay and wait to find out why she wasn't there.

"Where's Catherine?" whispered Benjamin.

"I've got no idea. I hope she's not sick." On the way to the meeting that morning, Samuel had told Benjamin everything that had happened the day before.

When the meeting was over, Samuel kept his distance from Catherine's parents, and when he saw them about to get in their buggy to go home he knew he had to say something. He said a quick prayer for God to help him.

He walked over to them just as they were both seated in the buggy, and called out, "Hello, Mr. Miller and Mrs. Miller."

Mr. Miller nodded his head to Samuel and got down from the buggy and his wife stayed seated. They were related twice by marriage, but by the look on his face, Samuel knew that this wasn't going to be a pleasant talk. Mr. Miller frowned and then opened his mouth to speak.

"Before you say anything, Mr. Miller, I just want to say I'm very sorry for bringing your *dochder* home like that. Nothing bad happened, I can assure you of that." He glanced over at Mrs. Miller. She could hear every word and her face was glum. "Is Catherine all right? Is she sick?"

"Samuel, Catherine is not allowed out of the house for three months. You need to understand that Catherine's *mudder* and I are protecting her."

"From me?"

"That's right. I don't know if something happened or if it didn't happen, but the way she came home is unacceptable."

He couldn't believe his ears that they thought Catherine had to be protected from him. Three months! It couldn't be true that he wouldn't see her for three whole months. He had to change their minds somehow. "I don't have any bad intentions toward her and nothing bad happened. She fell into the water and–"

"There's no need to say it all again. She came home a mess and I don't want to see that happen again."

"*Nee*, it won't happen again. It was an error in judgment that she put the dry clothes on. I didn't want her to catch a cold. Is she all right?"

"You're right about it being wrong. I'll not allow her out with you again."

Why was Mr. Fuller being like this? "Has someone said something bad about me?"

"I don't listen to rumors. I can tell you that Catherine won't be going out with you again and it was a mistake to allow it at all." Mr. Miller turned away from him and got back into his buggy.

Heartbroken, Samuel watched Catherine's father and mother drive away in their buggy. In time, he knew the Millers would know that he was a good person and only wanted the best for Catherine the same as they did. The only problem was, in the meantime he wouldn't be able to see her.

He looked around for Benjamin. His brother wasn't exactly the voice of reason or even someone who'd give him sympathy, but he was the only one apart from his mother who knew the situation. After working his way through the people still socializing, he found Benjamin and he was with Magnolia. Samuel couldn't stop smiling when he saw that Benjamin was doing his best to edge away from Magnolia, who was talking at ninety miles a minute. He made his way over to rescue his youngest brother.

CHAPTER 17

"Hı, Magnolia. Do you have any idea where Catherine is today?" If he let on that she was grounded then Magnolia would want to know why.

"Her *Mamm* said she was at home, but didn't say why. I was thinking of visiting her I have nothing else to do this afternoon."

"That would be *wunderbaar.*"

She eyed him strangely as though she knew something was going on. "Okay. What plans do you two have this afternoon?" She looked from one to the other.

"Nothing, I'm not doing anything," Samuel said. "I'll just be at home."

"Me too, I think. I'm having a rest before I have to start work tomorrow."

Magnolia laughed. "You sound like an old man, Benjamin."

"Why?"

"Why would you need to have a rest?"

"We work hard at the factory. Don't we, Samuel?"

Samuel nodded. "It's true. It's very tiring work."

"Hmm. Well, I'm going to visit Catherine and see why she didn't come. Her *mudder* didn't say she was sick or anything."

"Would you tell me what's wrong with her when you see her?" Samuel hoped he wasn't crossing the line. If he said much more …

"Sure. I'm guessing Catherine might fill me in." She tilted her chin upward.

"*Denke*, Magnolia. I sure would appreciate it." He realized that he had just given her an excuse to come to his house. That wasn't good for his brother. He glanced over at Benjamin. He couldn't even meet Magnolia anywhere to find out what happened because word would get out that they had met and that might get back to Catherine and she'd take it the wrong way.

Magnolia said, "I'll borrow a buggy. My aunt lets me borrow the old one whenever I want to get out."

"Perfect. Wait, could you take her a note from me?"

"Sure."

"Come with me. I'm sure I've got some paper in the buggy."

"I'll see you later this afternoon." Magnolia said smiling at Benjamin.

"We'll look forward to it," Benjamin smiled, and almost looked convincing.

As they walked to his buggy, Samuel said, "I really appreciate you doing this for me."

"No problem."

He reached his buggy, found paper and pen and scribbled the note. He rolled the paper and held it out toward her.

"Okay and don't worry, I won't read it." Magnolia giggled.

"I didn't think you would."

She closed the note tightly in her hand and hurried away.

When he got back to Benjamin, Samuel said, "You'll look forward to it?"

"What else could I say?"

"Nothing." Samuel hung his head. "Nothing would've been better. 'If you have nothing good to say, say nothing.' Right? You don't want to give her the wrong idea."

"It's too late for that. I'm sure she'd just make something up in her head anyway."

"Maybe." He stared at where Magnolia had gone and saw her talking to Mary Lou's parents. Hopefully, she was telling them of her plans for the afternoon and arranging to borrow a buggy.

Catherine had spoken to her parents briefly when they came home from the meeting and then she'd gone directly back to her room. She was upset with them and didn't see reason to be with them apart from being polite and saying hello when they returned from their morning meeting.

A little later on, Catherine heard Magnolia's voice downstairs and she listened hard. Her mother told her friend that she was grounded for three months, and then Magnolia asked if she was allowed to speak with her. Catherine held her breath and was delighted when Magnolia was told she could visit with her.

"Catherine, there's someone here to see you," her mother called out.

Catherine walked down the stairs and greeted Magnolia.

Catherine's mother came back in the room and spoke to Catherine. "Your *vadder* and I are going out this afternoon. We'll be back by supper."

Catherine gave a nod of acknowledgement, still unhappy with her parents and still not feeling like speaking to her mother.

As soon as the girls were by themselves, they sat in the living room. Catherine saw her quilt-in-progress in the corner of the room but she was too upset to sew.

"Why are you grounded?" Magnolia stared at her.

"I went out with Samuel yesterday and fell into the river. I came home with some dry clothes on and my hair was still a bit wet and my prayer *kapp* went missing. Nothing bad happened. It was all totally innocent. Samuel would never do anything bad."

"*Nee*, of course not and you couldn't help falling into the water and losing your prayer *kapp*."

Catherine was pleased her friend had no problem believing her. "It was so cold that Samuel suggested I get out of my wet clothes. He had some extra clothes, a spare set of his clothes, I mean, and I put them on so I wouldn't get pneumonia."

"You wore men's clothing and no prayer *kapp*?" Magnolia's eyebrows almost disappeared under the edge of her own *kapp*.

Catherine nodded. "I didn't have much choice. It was either that or stay in my freezing wet clothes."

"I can see why your folks were annoyed."

"It's not only that, they're worried about what happened with Timothy and they think that Samuel might do the same."

"What happened with Timothy?"

Catherine wasn't sure if Magnolia knew about Timothy. "Oh, nothing."

"You know?"

"*Jah*, do you?"

"*Jah*. I went with Mary Lou to Taylor's house when she invited Taylor to her wedding."

"Well my parents think less of Samuel's family now. I'm sure of it."

"That's not fair."

"I'm not sure, but that's what I think."

"Does Samuel know that you're grounded?"

"My *vadder* said he was going to find him and talk to him, so I guess he does by now."

Catherine asked, "Were you dating him—officially?"

"We went out once or twice."

Magnolia nodded. "I don't exactly call that dating. Do you want me to talk to Samuel for you and tell him what happened?"

"Would you?"

"*Jah.* I'll find him and tell him you're grounded, if he doesn't know. I was going to do something else today, but I don't mind going out of my way for you."

"*Denke,* Magnolia. You're a good friend. Lucy and Adeline are busy with their own lives at the moment. I've really had no one to talk with."

"Well, you've got me."

"I'm glad. I hope you don't go home too soon."

"Don't worry. I'm thinking of staying longer. At least until Mary Lou comes back home. Oh, I forgot. I have a note that he wrote. Wait here, I have it in the buggy." She came back and handed Catherine a folded paper.

Catherine placed it on the table, hoping it was from Samuel.

"Aren't you going to read it?"

"It's from Samuel?"

"*Jah,*" Magnolia nodded.

"Not right now. I'm too upset."

Magnolia reached for the letter. "Would you like me to read it to you?"

Catherine shook her head.

"Shall I take a message back to him for you?"

"Nee. I'm hoping time will sort this out."

Magnolia stood. "I should go."

"Already? You only just got here."

"I want to talk to Samuel and tell him how you are. He's really worried."

"Is he?"

"Jah."

Catherine nodded. "Tell him I'm okay."

SAMUEL WAS SITTING on the porch waiting for Magnolia. When he saw a horse and buggy approaching the house, he jumped to his feet. As she pulled up, he ran to the buggy.

"It's worse than I thought," Magnolia said as she jumped down. "She's grounded for three months. Can you believe it? I thought you should know."

"Did you give her my letter?"

"Jah, I did."

He held his breath waiting to hear Catherine's reaction, but Magnolia didn't speak. "And?"

"She didn't want to read it in front of me."

He was bitterly disappointed. "Can you take her another?"

"Today?"

He nodded.

"Sure."

"Can you wait right here? I'll go write a quick note to her."

Magnolia nodded again, and Samuel hurried away. He came back maybe ten minutes later with a sealed envelope. "You had no problem in seeing her?" he asked.

"Her *mudder* allowed me to visit, but she just can't go out." She looked around. "Where's Benjamin?"

"Asleep."

"Really?"

"*Jah.*"

"Um … do you want me to come back today?"

"Only if she writes a note back."

"Okay."

"*Denke*, Magnolia. I can't tell you how much I appreciate this."

"No worries."

CHAPTER 18

CATHERINE HAD BEGUN to sew her quilt, thinking that God would make a way for her to be with Samuel again soon. When she heard a horse, she hurried to the window and was surprised to see it was Magnolia again.

When she went out to meet her, Magnolia handed her a letter.

"From Samuel?"

"That's right, it's another one."

"Do you want *kaffe* or something?" Catherine clutched it in her hand.

"Jah, all this driving across the countryside has given me an appetite."

As they walked back into the house, Catherine said, "I think we have cake and cookies."

"Great."

"Which would you prefer?"

"Both."

Both girls sat drinking coffee and munching on cake and cookies with the sealed envelope in between them.

"Are you going to read it?"

Catherine breathed out heavily. "Not yet."

"Did you read the first one?" Magnolia asked.

"Not yet."

Magnolia sighed. "Why not?"

"I will, later."

"Read it while I'm here and I can take a letter back to him."

Catherine stared at the letter. She couldn't bring herself to look at it. No matter what it said it didn't make any difference if her parents wouldn't allow them to see each other. She couldn't go against them. All she could do was wait and pray, and then she knew they'd come around. "Not right now. I'll read it later."

"Okay, suit yourself."

"Take my mind off things and tell me what's been happening with you. You're staying here for longer than you thought you would be. Tell me why."

"I've always liked it here, in this community. Sometimes Mary Lou hasn't always been nice to me, but she's been good this time."

"Good. And what have you been doing?"

"I've been seeing a bit of Benjamin."

"As in going out with him, just the two of you, alone?"

Magnolia giggled. "Don't look so surprised."

"I am surprised because he is so much younger and … a little different than you. He's always goofing around and joking."

"I know what you mean. You think I should be with someone older and more serious."

She knew Magnolia was lying. "I think you should be with anyone you want. Whoever makes you happy. That's what I think." She stared at the letter from Samuel. "If only my parents thought the same way."

"I can see why they're so upset."

Catherine bit her lip. "I can too, but I explained everything that happened. Why can't they just trust me?"

"I think they do, but they are fearful of what could happen. It can't be easy being a parent and being responsible for another human life."

"I guess so. Thanks, you're making me feel much better."

"And you're teaching me to be a better sewer."

Catherine giggled. "I don't know about that. There's not much to sewing. It's just threading the needle and pushing it through the fabric."

"That's not so, I couldn't sew well until you showed me how. Now everything is so much easier."

"At least I've done something good with my life."

"Don't be like that. Things will work out. Do you want to write a letter back to Samuel? I'll take it to him if you want."

Once again, Catherine looked at the unopened envelope on the table. *"Nee denke.* I don't think I should reply."

"You haven't even read it yet."

"I'll read it later."

"Nee, I'll read it to you."

Catherine laughed. *"Nee,* that's fine. I'll read it later."

"Oh, sorry. I didn't realize that it could be personal."

"I don't know. It could be."

"He's probably apologizing for getting you into so much trouble."

"I don't know what's going on."

"Do you think your parents will let me visit again tomorrow?" Magnolia asked.

"I think so. Would you save me from going out of my mind?"

"I will. I enjoy my visits with you."

SAMUEL KEPT LOOKING out the window. Benjamin had left with his father to visit friends and Samuel and his mother were the only people home. Three hours had passed since he'd left the meeting. That was ample time for Magnolia to get to Catherine's place and then back to his place again. Of course, he'd told her she didn't need to come back if there wasn't a response from Catherine.

"Finally!" he yelled out when he saw a buggy

coming up the drive, driven by one person. When it got closer, he saw it was indeed Magnolia. He hoped that Catherine wasn't mad with him. After all, now she was grounded for months for what had happened while she was with him

He walked out to help Magnolia secure the horse.

"How was she?" he asked as he approached her.

"Miserable still."

"Is she mad with me?"

A pang stabbed through his stomach. "She's not pleased with you. Put it that way."

"Really? Did you give her my note?"

"Of course I did."

"And?"

She handed him a note. "She wrote one back to you."

"Denke." He was pleased to get something back from her and then realized he was being rude. "Come inside. *Mamm's* here and she'd love to make us a cup of hot tea or hot chocolate."

"I'd like that."

"Just don't tell her about the notes I wrote or about Catherine being grounded."

"I won't say anything."

They walked into the kitchen where Mrs. Fuller was already in the process of making hot chocolate.

"Hello, Magnolia. I saw you coming and thought you'd like a hot drink."

"*Denke.* I certainly would. Where's Benjamin? Has he gone out?"

"He went out with his *vadder.* It's about time the two of them did something together just the two of them," Mrs. Fuller said.

Magnolia pouted. "He said he'd be here resting."

"He probably didn't remember you were coming," Samuel said.

Magnolia sighed.

Halfway through their hot chocolates, Samuel left Magnolia with his mother and read the note.

He was surprised that Catherine's note said she didn't want to see him again, and he suddenly wondered if Magnolia had written it. Not wanting to accuse Magnolia of anything, he ignored his hunch and wrote to Catherine again and asked her to please forgive him. He told her that if he'd known she'd be grounded he would've insisted they come home directly. When he folded the note over, he sealed it in an envelope and went back to the kitchen.

Just as Magnolia was leaving, Samuel handed her the envelope. "Here's another letter. I really appreciate you doing this."

"I don't mind at all. This is what friends are for." She gave him a big smile. "It was really disappointing that Benjamin wasn't here."

He nodded. "I know. I will tell him you were looking for him."

"He could visit me at my place. My aunt and *onkel* wouldn't mind."

"I'll let him know." It was odd how she had become fixated on his younger brother.

"Do you mind if I give her this letter tomorrow?"

"That's fine. Whenever suits you. It doesn't have to be done today."

He watched as Magnolia got into her buggy and head down the driveway. The only question he had in his mind was how long would it take her to get the note to Catherine. Well, that and he wondered again who had written the note to him.

CHAPTER 19

IT WAS mid-morning Monday when Magnolia got to Catherine's house. Mrs. Miller was home, but she left the two young people in the living room to talk and sew together.

Magnolia slipped her the envelope first. "He really wants you to read this."

"Okay, *denke.*"

"Did you read the last one?"

"I put it away."

"You threw it away?" At that moment, they were interrupted by Catherine's mother telling them she was going out.

"Do you want me to hitch the buggy, *Mamm?*"

"*Nee,* you two girls stay inside. I can do it. I'm off to visit Lucy."

Catherine wondered if her mother was deliberately visiting Lucy today because she was grounded and

Mamm knew Catherine would've wanted to go with her.

When Mrs. Miller was out the door, Magnolia said, "Did you say you threw it out?"

"*Nee*, I just haven't read—"

"Don't you think you should read this one at least?"

"I will. Let's talk about something else."

"Okay I will put it here for you, but you better hide it before your mother gets home."

Catherine nodded and stared at the letter. She hated putting Samuel through this whole drama.

SAMUEL HEADED to his buggy after he finished work, and waiting by his buggy was Magnolia. "Hi, Magnolia."

"Hello. I have a note from Catherine."

"Oh good."

"I hope you think that once you've read it."

"Is she still upset with me?"

Magnolia shrugged. "I can't say."

Since it was a small folded-over piece of paper, he took it from her and silently read it while she was standing there. Besides, he figured, she'd probably already read it.

Dear Samuel,

I am grounded now because of you. Please just leave me alone.

Catherine

THAT WAS ALL? He couldn't believe that she wrote nothing else after the day they'd spent together. He looked up at Magnolia. "Was there anything else?"

"*Nee* there wasn't."

"Wait here and I'll write another. If you don't mind taking one to her again."

"I don't mind. I've got nothing better to do these days."

"I won't be long." He hurried back into the workshop to write another note.

CATHERINE,

I'm so sorry. Please forgive me. I've learned my lesson. So many bad things were done that day. it was the best day and also the worst day. The first part of the day was the best and then it turned into the worst. I don't know how. It must've come with those rain clouds and the breeze must've blown an ill wind. I don't know what I'll do if you don't forgive me. I've never felt like this about anyone before.

Samuel

HE SEALED IT IN AN ENVELOPE, took it outside and handed it to Magnolia.

"I'll take it to her tomorrow."

"Denke."

"Where's Benjamin?"

"He's inside working for a little longer today. Shall I call him out?"

"Nee, it's okay. Not if he's working." Magnolia got back into the buggy and drove away.

Right at that moment, and with the best timing in the world, Benjamin walked out of the workshop.

"You're not working late?"

"I was, but I just finished what I was working on. I thought you'd be gone."

"I was just talking to Magnolia. You just missed her."

Benjamin rolled his eyes.

"Don't be like that. She's helping me with Catherine."

"Let's go before she comes back." As they climbed into the buggy, Benjamin said, "I think you should speak to Mr. Miller."

"How can I? I can't go over there because of Catherine."

"Go to ... wherever he might be."

"I don't want to do that."

"Arrange to accidentally bump into him."

"Where?"

"Along the road near his house. It's fairly deserted and there won't be anyone around. You can wait up the road until you see his buggy coming and then wave him down and talk with him."

"That sounds like it might work. I only hope he stops."

"He'd have to. When will you do that?"

"I'll do it tomorrow afternoon." It was a little contrived, but desperate times called for desperate measures.

CHAPTER 20

AT LUNCHTIME THE NEXT DAY, Magnolia came into the factory and asked to speak with Samuel. He was surprised and walked outside to see her and she handed him another letter. He thanked her and read it in front of her.

DEAR SAMUEL,

Your last letter upset me. Why would you say it was a good day when it caused me to be stuck in the house? I don't want to see you again and I'm thinking of moving away to stay with Magnolia for a bit.

Catherine.

THEN SAMUEL KNEW in his heart that Magnolia had written the letter. This one, and the others.

"I can see that she doesn't want to see me again."

"Really? She doesn't want to see you again? That's too bad."

"Can you do something else for me, Magnolia?"

"Sure."

"I've hurt my hand at work and can't hold a pen. If I write a goodbye letter to Catherine, will you write what I tell you?"

"Okay."

He went into the office, came back out and handed her pen and paper and told her exactly what to write. When he saw her handwriting, he had proof. Magnolia was writing those letters and they weren't from Catherine at all. And … if she was substituting her letters, then she was most likely substituting his. What crazy things had Magnolia written to Catherine and had her thinking they were from him?

He grabbed the paper from her and ripped it in half. "On second thought, I'll not tell her anything."

"You're not going to break up with her?"

"I don't know yet."

"I haven't read her letters or yours, but from what you said, she's breaking up with you."

"I know. I need to think about things for a while." He turned and tossed the paper in the trash bin.

After Magnolia had left, he pulled the pieces of the letter out of the bin and compared that writing with the other letters supposedly from Catherine that he had tucked away in his buggy. Magnolia had tried to write differently but most of the Ys and the Ts were exactly the same, along with most of the Ss. Why was Magnolia interfering in their relationship and trying to tear them apart?

It was now more important than ever that he speak with Mr. Miller and somehow he had to let Catherine know that the letters were not from him.

Later that afternoon, while he was waiting for Mr. Miller, he realized he couldn't tell him about the fake letters Catherine had received without having to admit he was trying to write to her in secret when she was grounded. The only thing he could do was come clean —confess and risk Mr. Miller thinking less of him than he already did.

He sat there thinking how foolish he'd been to write the letters in the first place. It certainly was showing no respect for Mr. and Mrs. Miller while they were trying to protect their daughter.

When Samuel saw Mr. Miller's buggy, his heart sank. It could be years before the man forgave him for what he'd done, and would Catherine be willing to wait years for him?

He had precious little choice, though, and clicked his horse forward. When their buggies got close, he flagged Mr. Miller down.

"Hello, Samuel."

"Hello. Do you have a moment? I'd like to talk to you about something."

"You're not going to change my mind about Catherine being grounded."

"I'm not trying to talk you out of it. I have a confession to make, but not about what happened the other day. I already told you everything about that."

Mr. Miller frowned. "You have a confession about something else?"

"*Jah.*"

"We better get our buggies off the road then."

They pulled the buggies off on separate sides of the road and then Samuel hurried over to Mr. Miller's side.

"What is your confession?"

Samuel's mind went blank when he saw Mr. Miller's jaw tightened. "Um ..." He looked down at the ground and could feel Mr. Miller's eyes boring through him. He fought the fogginess in his mind. "When I took Catherine on the picnic, it happened just as I said, but when I found out she was grounded I couldn't bear not seeing or hearing from her for months. So, I did something that I shouldn't have." He shook his head feeling ashamed. "I had someone pass her notes."

Mr. Miller pushed out his lips. "The only person she's seen is Magnolia."

"It was Magnolia, but please don't blame her. It was me who was at fault."

"I'm glad you told me. *Denke.*"

"That's not all."

Mr. Miller stared at him. "You'd better tell me the rest."

"It's Magnolia. I'm not trying to get her into trouble, but I think everything should be out in the open. Hmm, I guess I should've spoken to her before I spoke to you."

"Go on."

"You see, she's been writing notes back to me as though they are from Catherine and those notes are telling me Catherine doesn't want to see me anymore. I compared her handwriting and they are definitely from Magnolia."

"If you hadn't written the notes behind our backs, you wouldn't have been deceived yourself."

Samuel nodded. "I've already thought of that. Are you able to tell Catherine what's happened?"

"I think we need to clear this up. I'll have Magnolia come to the house tomorrow at six, and if you can come at the same time, we'll clear this whole thing up so nothing is hidden."

"Me, come to the house?" He gulped, but the good thing was he'd see Catherine a whole lot sooner than he'd expected.

"That's right. It's the only way the truth can come out."

"Okay. I'll be there." Samuel headed back to his buggy feeling he'd done the right thing.

WHEN MR. MILLER CAME HOME, he told Catherine and his wife what Samuel had said. Mr. Miller said he was going to tell Mary Lou's parents that Magnolia was wanted at their house at six the next evening.

Catherine spent all the next day hoping that Magnolia wouldn't stop in at the house and ask why her parents wanted to see her that evening. She wouldn't have been able to say anything and that would've been an awkward situation. Thankfully, Magnolia didn't come there during the day. It wasn't going to be a pleasant evening, she thought, but at least she would get to see Samuel again.

"WHAT'S GOING ON, CATHERINE?" Magnolia asked when she walked into Catherine's home right at six o'clock.

Catherine felt awful for Magnolia because she was about to be very embarrassed. "It's about the letters."

"Samuel's letters?"

Catherine nodded.

Mr. Miller had everyone sit in the living room. He moved a couch, so that Mr. and Mrs. Miller could sit across from the younger people. Mr. Miller was first to talk. "Magnolia, Samuel has confessed to us that he asked you to pass letters to Catherine for him."

Her eyes grew wide and she glanced over at Samuel. "That's right. Am I in trouble?"

"It seems you have been replacing the true letters that Catherine wrote with ones in your own handwriting."

"Wait a minute," Catherine said. "That's not right. I never wrote any letters."

Samuel stared at Catherine. "I have letters from you."

"I wrote them," Magnolia said. "I only did it to save you both a lot of pain." She looked at Mr. Miller. "I could see the relationship between the two of them wasn't going to work, so I—"

"Tried to help it end faster?" Mrs. Miller crossed her arms and glared at Magnolia.

Catherine couldn't believe what she heard. "Magnolia, you wrote letters to Samuel and pretended they were from me?"

She nodded. "I did."

"So, you weren't replacing her letters," Samuel said, "You were just making up letters yourself and pretending they were from Catherine. And if you were doing that, what about the letters I wrote to Catherine?"

Catherine shrugged. "I couldn't open them. The whole thing just made me too upset. I always meant to open them, but I haven't yet."

"Catherine, perhaps you should give the letters back to Samuel to see if they are in his own hand?" Mrs. Miller suggested.

"Don't bother," Magnolia said. "Don't bother. I wrote them as well."

"Why would you do such a thing?" Catherine asked. "I thought you were my friend."

Magnolia turned her body to face Catherine. "I am your friend. But I didn't want to see you making a mistake."

"Are you calling Samuel a mistake?" Catherine asked.

"Perhaps I should leave now," Samuel said.

Magnolia flew to her feet. "I will go. What I did was wrong, but I did it for the right reasons. No need to tell anyone. I'm leaving this community and I won't be coming back." Magnolia stomped to the door and turned around when she reached it. "Some people just don't appreciate what you do for them." Then, she walked out without saying anything further.

"I'm in shock," Catherine said.

"Me too," added Mrs. Miller.

Catherine turned to Samuel. "How did you discover what she was up to?"

"Just a feeling at first, and then I had her write something for me when she delivered one of the letters to me. I recognized the handwriting. The letters said you didn't want to see me again, or words to that effect."

Catherine gasped and then looked at her parents. "Are you going to tell the bishop?"

Mrs. Miller said, "*Nee,* no harm's been done and she feels bad enough about it that she's leaving."

"I feel sad for her, but at the same time … I can't believe what she's done. Mary Lou will wonder why she's not here when she gets back. Magnolia told Mary

Lou she had decided to stay longer. I wonder what excuse she'll give her for leaving so quickly."

"I'm sure she'll be able to come up with something," Samuel said.

"And as for you, young man …"

Samuel stared at Mr. Miller waiting for what he had to say. *"Jah?"*

"Catherine's mother and I have decided that since you've confessed your wrongdoing, we both trust that what you and Catherine told us about the river incident could be the truth."

"Is the truth," Mrs. Miller corrected.

"It is," Catherine said.

Mr. Miller turned to Catherine. "I haven't finished yet. Since we're both prepared to believe the pair of you, Catherine will no longer be grounded."

Catherine could barely contain her excitement and she looked across at Samuel. Now they could take up where they had left off.

"Just be careful. Okay?"

"Jah, Mr. Miller. I will … we will. I'm just glad that things are back to normal. *Denke,* for forgiving us, and for trusting us about what happened the other day," Samuel said to Mr. and Mrs. Miller.

"She's our youngest *dochder* and she's special to us," Mrs. Miller explained.

"Her *mudder* is more protective of the last to leave her nest." Mr. Miller gave a little chuckle.

"Aw, *Mamm.* I'm not that young."

"I completely understand," Samuel said, glad that he was going to be able to spend time with Catherine without having to wait for months. "Might I be able to call on Catherine tomorrow afternoon?"

"It's up to Catherine," Mr. Miller said.

Catherine nodded. *"Jah,* I'd like that."

"I'll come right after work."

"Okay."

Mrs. Miller said, "You both showed poor judgement, but in the end, I think you've both learned a good lesson."

Samuel nodded. "We have." He smiled at Catherine and then stood. "I should go. It's been quite a night."

To his disappointment, Mr. Miller walked him to the door rather than Catherine.

When Samuel arrived home and walked in the door of his house, he heard Timothy, the brother who was on *rumspringa,* talking to his mother in the kitchen.

"The girl isn't going to leave her family," their mother said.

"She's asking questions. Isn't that *gut, Mamm?"*

Samuel crept past the kitchen and headed up the stairs. He'd had enough conflict for one lifetime. Timothy being there was a good sign and from what he had said to *Mamm,* he was keeping in touch with Taylor. Things were improving, and for his brother to be talking with their mother was also a giant leap.

WHEN MARY LOU came home from her brief post-wedding vacation, her mother told her that Magnolia had left quickly and that it had something to do with Catherine.

Mary Lou didn't want to ask Catherine directly what conflict there had been between her and Magnolia, so she paid Catherine a casual visit.

As they sat in the living room, they talked about Mary Lou's wedding. Then Mary Lou turned the conversation in a different direction. "I hear you and Samuel are now dating. My new *mudder*-in-law couldn't wait to tell me."

Catherine giggled. "I have you to thank for that."

"Me?"

"Do you want me to tell you how I knew *Gott* had Samuel chosen for me?"

"Tell me."

"I was praying to *Gott* to find me a man—someone whom I would marry. I didn't want to go out with a lot of men. I just wanted to go out with someone and have that be the person I married. It was when you and Magnolia came to my *haus* some weeks ago. You didn't stay long, and you both kept talking about Samuel."

"I don't think I said anything about Samuel."

"It might have been just Magnolia. Anyway, before that I hadn't thought about Samuel in that way."

Mary Lou had a hard time absorbing the information. Her plan of matching Magnolia with Samuel had backfired. "And you thought that was God showing—"

"It had to have been. Don't you think?"

Mary Lou shrugged her shoulders.

Catherine smiled. "So, I owe it all to you and Magnolia, and to *Gott*, of course."

"Hmm. I suppose that's good. So, you're not mad with her anymore?"

"*Nee.* I never was mad. I was shocked that she'd do what she did. Oh, do you know?"

Mary Lou nodded. "What part of it was the most distressing for you?"

"All of it really. I couldn't believe that she gave letters to Samuel that I hadn't even written, and that she pretended I was telling him I wanted to break up with him. Or that she would be so bold as to follow us that first time when we went out to the café."

Mary Lou slowly nodded. Now that she had that much information, she could find out the rest from Magnolia. Even before she'd turned her new leaf, she wouldn't have done anything so devious.

"Do you think I should write to her?"

"I'll handle it. She likes it here, but she won't come back if she thinks everyone hates her."

"No one does. It's only Samuel and my folks who know what happened. No one's going to hold it against her."

"*Denke,* Catherine. I'll let her know."

CHAPTER 21

ON THE NEXT FRIDAY NIGHT, Samuel collected Catherine after he got off work to have a quiet dinner together.

As Samuel moved onto the road, he said, "A storm's coming."

She looked out at the sky.

He continued, "Jacob told me that Mary Lou has invited Magnolia back and she's coming."

"Oh, is that what you meant about a storm coming?" Catherine asked. "I'd heard that from Mary Lou, too."

He chuckled. *"Nee,* look over there." He pointed to the far right where gray clouds gathered, while he moved his horse down the driveway.

"Mary Lou told me she contacted her because she felt bad for her over what happened with the letters."

"It's not pleasant. I don't even know if Magnolia realizes she did a bad thing."

"I'm sure she does and she's very embarrassed and humiliated. At least she admitted it."

Samuel chuckled. "You always see the best in everyone."

"Well, not really. I remember Mary Lou did ..."

"What?"

"Nothing. Forget it." Catherine remembered how Mary Lou was horrible to her sisters some time ago, but it wasn't nice to talk about her behind her back.

"Tell me," Samuel urged.

"It's just that Mary Lou wasn't always how she is now. She changed."

"Maybe Magnolia will change too."

Catherine nodded. "I hope so."

"We'll soon see because she's coming back in a few months' time. Let's not let her come between us."

"You think she could?"

"She tried once. I don't want her to give it another shot."

"Me either. I don't think there would be anything she could do or say that would come between us," Catherine said.

He took his eyes off the road ahead and glanced at her. "Especially not when we marry."

She stared at him. "Marry?"

"Will you?"

"Will I?"

"Marry me?"

She giggled nervously. It was the best thing she'd ever heard in her life.

"What do you say?" He stopped the buggy on the edge of the road, turned and stared into her eyes.

"Do we know each other well enough?" she asked.

"Jah. I know that I want to marry you. You're perfect."

"I'm not perfect, but you are."

He chuckled. "I'm not. Not at all. Your *vadder* can tell you that."

She laughed for joy. All her dreams, hopes and prayers had come true. He was looking at her, waiting for an answer. "I will."

"You mean it?"

"Jah."

He grabbed hold of her hand, kissed it, and then she leaned over and kissed him on his cheek.

"When shall we tell our folks?" she asked.

Samuel grimaced. "That's something I'm not looking forward to."

"They've put all that behind them. Oh, and what did you do with my wet clothes? I keep forgetting to ask."

"They're in the back of the buggy. I keep forgetting to give them to you. *Mamm* washed them and ironed them."

"That's embarrassing."

"She understood perfectly when I told her what happened."

"She has always been nice to me."

He chuckled. "It is rather funny that your two sisters have married two of my older brothers."

"Jah, I know. It's nice."

He smiled at her. "You're nice."

"So are you." She looked into his warm brown eyes and felt dizzy. God had answered her prayers and she would thank him daily.

"I have land, and now we just need to build a *haus.*"

"We?"

Samuel chuckled. "My brothers and I will build it. You can do the work of helping me design it."

"I'll have no problem doing that."

"Let's go and tell them right now."

"My parents?"

"Jah."

Catherine took a deep breath. "Okay."

A few minutes later, they were back at Catherine's house sitting in front of her parents.

Samuel drew in a deep breath.

"Catherine and I are … Myself and …" He looked at Catherine and she nodded giving him encouragement. "Catherine has agreed …"

Catherine's mother grinned as she leaped to her feet. "You're getting married?"

Catherine jumped up, too. *"Jah, Mamm."* Catherine's mother grabbed her in a bear hug.

Mr. Miller stood up and put his hand out to

Samuel, who stood and then shook his future father-in-law's hand. "We thought this was coming."

After Catherine and her father hugged, Mr. Miller took the opportunity to pull Samuel to one side to have a quiet word to him. They stepped into the cool of the night to talk on the porch. Samuel hoped that Mr. Miller wasn't having second thoughts on him marrying Catherine. They walked together to the end of the porch before Catherine's father spoke a word.

"I just want to say that Catherine's mother and I are very happy at the idea of having you for a son-in-law."

Samuel could see the sincerity in his face and the sincere manner in which he uttered the words carried a great deal of weight. *"Denke.* That means a great deal. I will look after her. I'm a hard worker and I'll always provide for her."

Mr. Miller's face broke into a smile as he patted Samuel on his back. "I should never have doubted you, but I was worried with Timothy, and all."

"I thought that might have troubled you, but anyone can make a mistake. My brothers' choices are no reflection on my own. I am a separate person to the others in my family, yet ..." Samuel gulped. In the past, being a Fuller meant being trustworthy and reliable. With Timothy getting an *Englisch* girl pregnant, that reputation was tainted. "In the past ..."

"Nothing needs to be said."

"Jah, it does. I often don't say much and I'm not as good at talking as I'd like to be, but I have to tell you

that doing anything disrespectful toward Catherine when she fell in the river never entered my mind. I was concerned only for her health. I've always wanted Catherine as my *fraa* and have looked at no other girl in the same way. I wouldn't jeopardise our future by making advances. That's not in my nature."

Mr. Miller stared at him. "I know that now, and that's why I'm happy you're marrying Catherine. The two of you will make a good life together. The other thing I wanted to mention is have you given much thought to where you'll be living after you're married?"

"I bought land when I was seventeen."

"A smart move."

"I got it for a good price and paid it off a long time ago. My brothers will help me build the *haus.* I'm hoping Catherine won't mind living with my parents for about six months during the building process."

Mr. Miller rubbed his beard. "Could the two of you stay here for that six months? I know Catherine's *mudder* would like it."

Samuel smiled. "It is a little closer to work."

"We'll give you your privacy as much as we can."

"*Denke.* I'll organize that. *Mamm's* got Benjamin left at home, and all the problems with Timothy to work through. She might be pleased to be rid of me, but maybe a little sad not having Catherine there, of course. She always hoped for a *dochder,* but *Gott* gave her a houseful of boys instead."

Mr. Miller chuckled. "I hope everything works itself out with Timothy, and that he comes back to us."

"I'm sure it will work out."

"I won't mention a thing to Catherine. I'll let you work it out between you, your *mudder* and Catherine."

"*Denke.* I appreciate that."

"I'll fetch Catherine. She'll be worried about what I wanted to say to you."

"You had me a little worried too."

Mr. Miller shook his hand again, and then as soon as he opened the door, Catherine burst through it.

"*Gut nacht, Dat.* Don't wait up." She breezed past her father, and then grabbed Samuel and linked her arm through his. "Let's go."

By the time her father said goodnight, they were climbing into the buggy.

"Your *Dat* said ..."

"I heard what he said. He's got a loud voice. I couldn't help overhearing, and I don't care where we live as long as I'm with you." She moved closer and put her head on his shoulder.

"Then I think we should live with your folks until the *haus* is built. *Mamm's* got a lot on her mind, and we can visit there as often as we want."

"Okay."

UNAWARE THAT SAMUEL was proposing to Catherine

right at that moment, Mary Lou was fixing the evening meal for Jacob and herself. She was feeling pleased that *Gott* had used her to bring Catherine and Samuel together. She was certain *Gott* had a sense of humor with how it had all played out.

She felt sorry enough for Magnolia that she'd even invited her to stay with her and Jacob at their new home. She felt a little to blame when she heard about the whole thing with the letters. After all, she'd told Magnolia that she thought Samuel liked her. It must've been hard for Magnolia to watch everyone pair up while she was left alone, passed over every time. There must be a man out there somewhere for Magnolia. A man who would overlook what she was like. *There's a lid for every pot,* her grandmother always used to say.

One thing Mary Lou wanted to accomplish before Taylor and Timothy's baby was born was to bring the two of them together. She'd make that her new mission in life.

$\sim$

WITH CATHERINE by Samuel's side and about to become his wife, Samuel had everything he had ever wanted. He'd planned his life from the time he was sixteen. He'd scraped and saved to buy several acres of land to build a home for his future family. Now, that land was worth a whole lot more than he'd paid and soon he'd see a house rising on it. He envisioned gardens for food and flowers, and a barn and horse pastures. His hopes and plans were being realized, but from now on he and Catherine would be making plans together.

One thing that had been out of Samuel's control was love. He could buy a piece of land, but finding a *fraa* was an entirely different matter. That was in God's hands. Being older than Catherine, Samuel had watched her grow from a vibrant girl into a kind and thoughtful young woman. He'd prayed for Catherine to notice him, and God had smiled on them both and worked another miracle.

❧

❧

Thank you for reading The Quiet Amish Bachelor. I do hope you enjoyed it.
Samantha Price

The next books in the series are:
Book 6 The Determined Amish Bachelor
Book 7 Amish Bachelor's Secret

Previous books in the SEVEN AMISH BACHELORS series.
Book 1 The Amish Bachelor
Book 2 His Amish Romance
Book 3 Joshua's Choice
Book 4 Forbidden Amish Romance

IF YOU'D LIKE to be notified of my new releases, special offers and occasional freebies, add your email at the 'mailing list' area of my website: www.samanthapriceauthor.com

Book 9 Amish Widow's Secret

Book 10 The Middle-Aged Amish Widow

Book 11 Amish Widow's Escape

Book 12 Amish Widow's Christmas

Book 13 Amish Widow's New Hope

Book 14 Amish Widow's Story

Book 15 Amish Widow's Decision

AMISH LOVE BLOOMS

Book 1 Amish Rose

Book 2 Amish Tulip

Book 3 Amish Daisy

Book 4 Amish Lily

Book 5 Amish Violet

Book 6 Amish Willow

AMISH BRIDES

Book 1 Arranged Marriage

Book 2 Falling in Love

Book 3 Finding Love

Book 4 Amish Second Loves

Book 5 Amish Silence

ETTIE SMITH AMISH MYSTERIES (Cozy Mystery series)

Book 1 Secrets Come Home

Book 2 Amish Murder

Book 3 Murder in the Amish Bakery

Book 4 Amish Murder Too Close

Book 5 Amish Quilt Shop Mystery

Book 6 Amish Baby Mystery

Book 7 Betrayed

Book 8 Amish False Witness

Book 9 Amish Barn Murders

Book 10 Amish Christmas Mystery

Book 11 Who Killed Uncle Alfie?

Book 12 Lost: Amish Mystery

Book 13 Amish Cover-Up

Book 14 Amish Crossword Murder

AMISH TWIN HEARTS

Book 1 Amish Trading Places

Book 2 Amish Truth Be Told

Book 3 The Big Beautiful Amish Woman

Book 4 The Amish Widow and the Millionaire

AMISH ROMANCE SECRETS

ABOUT THE AUTHOR

Samantha Price is a best selling author who knew she wanted to become a writer at the age of seven, while her grandmother read to her Peter Rabbit in the sun room. Though the adventures of Peter and his sisters Flopsy, Mopsy, and Cotton-tail started Samantha on her creative journey, it is now her love of Amish culture that inspires her to write. Her writing is clean and wholesome, with more than a dash of sweetness. Though she has penned over eighty Amish Romance and Amish Mystery books, Samantha is just as in love today with exploring the spiritual and emotional journeys of her characters as she was the day she first put pen to paper. Samantha lives in a quaint Victorian cottage with three rambunctious dogs.

Follow Samantha Price on BookBub
www.samanthapriceauthor.com
samanthaprice333@gmail.com
www.facebook.com/SamanthaPriceAuthor
Twitter @ AmishRomance

16333122R00106

Made in the USA
Middletown, DE
23 November 2018